Love with the perfect stranger

Eve kept her eyes closed, almost afraid of what she would find when she opened them. She felt a kiss on her cheek, then at the corner of her lips.

Max wasn't going to go away.

She let out a long, slow breath as she gazed up at him. Then she took another and let it out. Slowly. What did one say after an incredible lovemaking experience like *that?*

He touched his forehead to hers, and looked so touchingly, achingly vulnerable that her throat constricted.

"Ho, ho, ho," he whispered, then kissed her again.

Laughter bubbled up inside her, wonderful laughter, and she realized she'd never really laughed in bed with a man before.

"Merry Christmas," she whispered, then for some insane reason erupted into another gale of giggles.

"And what would you like in your stocking, little girl?" He was already hard again, and she caught her breath.

Max was the most exciting Christmas present she'd ever had!

With over a decade's success in contemporary and historical romance fiction, award-winning author **Elda Minger** is known and loved for her emotionally charged and sensuous stories. "Love is the most powerful and healing force on earth," she says. "I consider it both an honor and a privilege to be working in this genre." An avid reader, Elda writes what she loves to read. Her passions also include "The X-Files," travel and chocolate in any form. Watch for her next exciting Temptation novel, *Night Rhythms,* in the summer of 1997. Enjoy!

Books by Elda Minger

HARLEQUIN TEMPTATION
590—THE LAST SEDUCTION

HARLEQUIN AMERICAN ROMANCE
469—BRIDE FOR A NIGHT
489—DADDY'S LITTLE DIVIDEND
510—WED AGAIN
531—TEDDY BEAR HEIR
584—BABY BY CHANCE

Elda Minger
CHRISTMAS WITH EVE

Harlequin Books

TORONTO • NEW YORK • LONDON
AMSTERDAM • PARIS • SYDNEY • HAMBURG
STOCKHOLM • ATHENS • TOKYO • MILAN
MADRID • WARSAW • BUDAPEST • AUCKLAND

To Birgit Davis-Todd, for a gorgeous cover, the
inspiration of a pair of red satin pajamas, and a very
clever title. You are a joy to work with!

ISBN 0-373-25714-7

CHRISTMAS WITH EVE

Copyright © 1996 by Elda Minger.

1

"YOU'RE SURE YOU DON'T want to join us, Professor Vaughn? It's going to be a terrific Christmas party."

Eve looked up from her desk at the young woman poised in her office doorway. Shelley, one of her college students, had the requisite long straight hair, faded jeans, bulky Irish knit sweater and leather backpack. The concerned expression on her face touched Eve. Shelley looked so very young.

"Thank you for the invitation, but I'm driving in to Columbus to spend Christmas Eve with a friend."

"Oh." Eve could tell from the interested look in Shelley's brown eyes that she wondered if this friend was a man.

"My college roommate," Eve said, and watched the speculation fade from the young woman's eyes.

"Well, then, have a Merry Christmas and I'll see you next semester. I'm signed up to take your advanced seminar on human sexuality."

"I'm glad."

Shelley bounded out of the office with youthful energy. At thirty-three, Eve was only fourteen years older than her student, but every year weighed heavily upon her.

Christmas Eve. A time for family. And she had none.

Her mother had been her only family, and Mary Anne Vaughn had died almost eighteen months ago. Eve was an only child, and had grown up with no father to speak of. She and her mother had always been close, but had never smothered each other. Rather, they had been two women with a biological bond who also happened to genuinely enjoy each other's company.

That first Christmas had been hard. This one promised to be just as difficult.

Eve stared out the window at the bare branches of the large oak tree outside her office window. She loved teaching at Middleton University, but there were times—and Christmas vacation was one of them—when she was sharply reminded of what her life lacked.

Gail, her college roommate, had called over a month ago and asked her to spend the holidays in Columbus with her and her husband. And their new baby. Eve had declined at first, making up some dim excuse about a heavy work load. But Gail knew her. She'd gently encouraged her, and Eve had finally agreed.

She should be getting ready to go right now, instead of staring out the window and procrastinating, she chided herself.

So she started for home, leaving the old brick building that housed the psychology department. The winter wind was bitterly cold, as cold as it always was in central Ohio. The campus was deserted, most of the students already home for the holidays. The few that had elected to stay over for the duration of the vacation, like Shelley, were anticipating the various dorm parties they'd planned.

Eve lived on campus, within walking distance of the faculty building. Her house, set back among a grove of birch trees, was small but cozy. She'd taken great pains to make her house a home. All blond wood and glass inside, it was furnished in a modern, contemporary style. Very spare. But the huge windows facing the woods gave the place its real charm.

For a moment, as she stepped inside the quiet house, she contemplated simply lighting a fire, pouring herself a glass of good red wine, calling Gail and attempting to beg off the entire evening. Perhaps it was her mother's death. Perhaps it was because Christmas had always been her parent's favorite holiday. Mary Anne had gone all out and made Christmas so very special, every single year.

Aside from reminiscing about her mother, Eve had noticed a brooding quality to her thoughts lately. She had been pondering on the direction her life had taken, and wasn't sure she liked it.

More than anything, she wasn't sure she would be able to spend Christmas Eve with her friends without looking at their baby and bursting into tears.

So broody. What's the matter with me?

Her cat, Caliban, ran into the room and twined his slender body around her legs, purring loudly. The sound broke the silence of the room.

"Hey, Callie." Eve pulled off her outerwear, then picked up the elegant black feline and walked with him to the kitchen.

Leaving Caliban a bowl overflowing with dry cat food and another filled with plenty of water, she headed upstairs where her suitcase was already packed and ready to go. Presents for Gail and her family were in the trunk of her car, and had been since earlier in the month.

If only she wasn't filled with such a sense of dread.

THE STORM STARTED when she was only twenty minutes away from campus. Thick flurries of snowflakes flew across the gray, leaden sky. The dark blue Volvo she drove had a terrific heater; she even had the option of warming the driver's seat. But it still seemed so cold.

She knew dusk was a dangerous time to be driving. Why she hadn't started out this morning when the sky had been a clear, crystalline blue she didn't know.

Actually she did. She didn't want to go. Christmas was hard for her. She didn't want to be alone any longer—but she didn't know how to correct the situation.

She knew, from her study of psychology, that one couldn't judge one's own insides by other people's outsides. No matter how effortlessly everyone else on the planet seemed to pair up and reproduce, she knew that they all had the same problems, that no one's life was perfect.

It just seemed that hers was missing so much.

The thought of dating was horrifying. She knew that her attitude sounded like something out of a woman's magazine. *All the good ones are taken. Men don't seem to want to commit these days. Married women are more depressed than single women, while single men are more depressed than married men. With a divorce rate of over fifty percent, marriage is an outmoded system. It obviously doesn't work for women, and is more of a support system for men.* On and on and on . . .

Actually, Eve could sum up her entire problem in a nutshell.

The bottom line is that you're lonely. And scared. And don't have a whole lot of experience dealing with this sort of thing.

She concentrated on steering her car over a particularly slippery stretch of the interstate. All around her, other cars were skidding and sliding. When she saw a red station wagon fishtail across the highway and slide off on to the shoulder, she made up her mind.

This was not smart.

She got off at the next exit, the snow coming down in flurries so thick, she couldn't even see the name of the exit. Driving as slowly as she dared, squinting to see through the windshield, her wipers going at full speed, Eve decided that the first motel or hotel she found, no matter how squalid or depressing, was where she was going to spend Christmas Eve.

It couldn't possibly be worse than last year's disaster. She'd tried her best to re-create what her mother had usually done, and failed miserably. Her homemade wreath had ended up looking like Charlie Brown's Christmas tree. The gingerbread men had burned to a crisp, and her hot cider simply hadn't tasted the same. It had all fallen flat, and she'd gone off to bed feeling miserable.

The loneliness had been overwhelming, and Eve had resolved after that experience to never celebrate Christmas again. A tad dramatic at the time, but she'd been feeling awful.

As she entered the small town, she passed a gas station, all decked out with Christmas lights, a huge wreath on the door. A video store, a minimart, then houses. Homes trimmed with sparkling lights, displaying carefully decorated trees in the windows.

Where families were gathered to spend the holiday together.

Eve kept driving, feeling slightly safer off the highway. The car was warm, she had almost a full tank of

gas and if worse came to worst, she could circle back
to the all-night minimart, park in the driveway, mi-
crowave a hot dog for Christmas Eve dinner and sleep
in the car. She'd even have hot coffee the following
morning. And a cheese Danish.

This was getting really depressing.

Snap out of it. Now.

She turned right, then left, through what she supposed passed for a downtown. Then she noticed that
the main street was heading straight back to the interstate.

Eve was just about to turn back toward the minimart when a house caught her eye. Although barely
visible through flurries of snow, the yellow Victorian
still managed to put everyone else's decorations to
shame.

The evergreen trees out front were adorned with
small, twinkling white lights. A large bay window
displayed an enormous blue spruce, crammed with
decorations and lights. This was the type of home
whose door would sport a sheaf of wheat in the fall,
a cluster of pussy willows in the spring. And a huge
evergreen wreath with a red velvet bow at Christ-
mastime.

I want to move in with these people.

The thought was totally irrational, but the house
exuded happiness. Eve slowed her car as she passed
the cheerful structure, wondering if she dared ask the
people who lived there if they knew of a decent place

to stay. A hot dog at a minimart on Christmas Eve was too low for even her to sink.

Then she noticed the sign. Swan's Bed And Breakfast.

Perfect.

She parked her car, grabbed her purse. Bracing herself against the snow and frigid air, she let herself out of the warmth of her Volvo and struggled up the slippery front steps of the yellow Victorian. If they didn't have a room, she'd sleep on the couch in the living room, right by the Christmas tree, like a little kid awaiting the arrival of Santa Claus.

The foyer was lovely, decorated in a country style but not so overcluttered that you were tripping over doorstops and crashing into baskets. She could smell the wonderful, cinnamony fragrance of Christmas potpourri, overlaid with the scents of roasting turkey, sage, onions, gingerbread—

Perfect.

Eve could hear the sound of someone playing Christmas carols on a piano. Fragrant greens and bright bows were everywhere. Glitter-wrapped gifts sat waiting beneath an enormous, Victorian fantasy tree. Every windowsill sported a nutcracker, a reindeer, an angel or a poinsettia. Candles, all of them lit against the dusk, flickered warmly. Even the staircase was adorned with ribbons and cedar branches.

Someone had taken the time to create Christmas. Someone very like her mother. Eve could feel herself start to relax. Now, if only there was a vacancy—

When an elderly man approached her and introduced himself as the owner, she quickly inquired. Yes, there was a room. She whipped out her credit card. The owner's college-age grandson offered to go get her bag out of the trunk of her car. She was tired and gratefully accepted. As soon as she entered her room, she called Gail, who was glad to hear she was off the road and in a warm, safe place.

"It's supposed to storm for the next few days. A real blizzard."

"I'm sorry," Eve said, and found that she meant it. Now that there was no chance of her spending Christmas with her friend, she found that she regretted the strange turn of events.

"No, don't worry," said Gail. "I'm just glad you found a place to stay. But as soon as the weather lets up, I want you to come down and see us."

"I will."

Her room was on the second floor. Situated at the back of the large house, it overlooked the woods and the now-frozen garden. Someone had built a snowman, with a large carrot nose. Little balls of suet and birdseed hung on several of the trees. She'd bet whoever had done that had also remembered nuts for the squirrels.

Peaceful. The bedroom was peaceful. Decorated in shades of blue and mauve, with a canopied four-poster bed. Eve ran her fingers over the down comforter, admired the lace-trimmed linens. A mountain of pillows was piled on the bed. A comfy chair, with a hand-knit afghan draped across it, sat in the corner. An excellent reading lamp stood beside it, tempting Eve to sink into the chair and forget all her troubles.

All I need is a good book and some chocolate....

There was even a fireplace, with logs and kindling already laid. A giant Christmas wreath hung over that same fireplace, decorated with gingerbread boys and swirls of red velvet ribbon.

Perhaps you could order up a glass of wine....

Eve was charmed by the little goody bag on the night table, containing gumdrops, expensive chocolates and a small bag of the fragrant house potpourri. On impulse, she opened the drawer and found several current best sellers.

What thoughtful hosts....

She was examining the small topiary rosemary bush shaped like a tiny Christmas tree on the bureau when a knock on the door startled her. The owner's grandson, with her bag, and his sister behind him, with a plate of fragrant ginger cookies and rich, chocolate brownies, obviously straight from the oven, along with a mug of hot cider.

"Grandma thought you looked a little cold," the girl explained. Eve simply melted. She thanked them both, overtipping them. They smiled.

"Dinner's in about an hour," the young man said. "But we're having drinks in the parlor."

Drinks in the parlor. She liked the sound of that.

"I'll be right down."

She took a quick shower, washing away all the tension of the drive with the all-natural citrus bath gel she found in a wicker basket. The towels were cotton and thick, the basket by the sink filled with organic bubble bath, body lotions and shampoos.

Eve dressed in the outfit she'd packed for Christmas Day at Gail's—a hunter green velvet dress that was the perfect match for her dark auburn hair.

Strangely enough, it was beginning to feel a lot like Christmas. The element of the unexpected that this day held, the sense of not knowing what lay just around the corner. Driving out of the storm, finding this house. Falling in love with it and then discovering that she could purchase an evening inside its walls, even pretend for a while that she lived here. The day had become full of delightful surprises.

She liked it. She liked feeling this way. Everything about this vacation, everything about her life, had seemed as if it were going to be predictable. Now circumstances had made her stray from her planned route, and Eve found herself intrigued.

It was like . . . waiting for Santa.

Quickly applying some makeup and arranging her shoulder-length hair into some semblance of order, she slipped on her heels, grabbed her room key, then headed out the door.

MAX SAW HER the minute she entered the room.

It certainly wasn't as if he were on the prowl for feminine companionship. He'd come to this particular bed and breakfast at the suggestion of a friend, to enjoy a relaxed holiday before starting his new job. The next year promised to be a hectic one, and though he liked working hard, he also knew the value of relaxation.

She danced into the room, radiating high spirits. He simply stared. She was petite, with dark auburn hair that picked up the lights. She'd left it sort of wild, and he liked that, liked the thought that she might be a woman given to a little wildness. He couldn't see the color of her eyes, not from this distance, but he'd bet they were green.

And that dress. Dark green velvet, it caressed a tiny, but curvy figure. Terrific cleavage. Great legs.

He smiled, then glanced up, looking for mistletoe.

She waltzed—and there was no other word for it— up to the bartender and he heard her voice as she asked him for a glass of red wine. Low and melodic. Expressive. He thought of that voice in the dark, those lips against his ear, what she'd tell him to do—

The bartender talked her out of the red wine and into a spiced rum punch.

Max liked that, as well. *So, the lady can be persuaded.* He knew what he wanted to talk her into, but he wouldn't rush things. They had all the time in the world. In this blizzard, no one would be going anywhere soon.

He watched her as she took her drink and walked over to one of the large bay windows. As she glanced around the decorated room, she took delight in everything. Everywhere she looked, something caught her eye, made her smile.

He took delight in her.

Something he couldn't put his finger on, something in the way she was, moved him. He was so used to being around people who had already decided, in their twenties and thirties, that to show delight in anything was the height of unsophistication. He'd never liked that philosophy. As a scientist, he took delight in discovery each and every day.

He guessed her to be in her late twenties. He wondered what in God's name she was doing here all alone. Why would a woman like this be alone on Christmas Eve? What kind of fool, specifically what kind of *masculine* fool, would allow her to spend the holidays by herself?

Perhaps she got caught in the storm. Maybe she has a family at home, he reasoned with himself.

Some family, if the thought of being alone at this inn has her lighting up like the Christmas tree out front...

He moved closer, checked her left hand. No ring.

The sense of relief that discovery created startled him. No stranger to the ways of male-female courtship, Max knew he had it bad. Over the moon. Hit by lightning.

Now, it was only a matter of getting to know her.

"BUT I DIDN'T ORDER another drink," Eve protested as the bartender made his way toward her, a second rum punch in hand.

"You didn't." He grinned. "That man over there did."

She glanced up and saw him. Wondered how in the world she'd missed him among the twenty or so people. Tall. Brown hair. Striking good looks. She couldn't see the color of his eyes at this distance, but she'd bet they were blue.

He was dressed in jeans, boots, a blue shirt and a tweedy jacket. His looks cataloged him as a young professional. The look he was giving her left no doubt as to what was on his mind.

Driven by the way this extraordinary day had been unfolding, Eve did exactly the opposite of what she would ordinarily do.

She smiled at him.

Within seconds, he was at her side.

"Green. Just as I thought," he said.

"What?" She liked his voice. It was dark, deep, thoroughly masculine. But it had a slightly sandpapery quality to it, like he'd just rolled out of bed. He reminded her of an actor she'd seen in some movie, but she couldn't think of his name.

"Your eyes. I thought they'd be green."

Blue, she thought as she looked up at him. His eyes were dark blue. Bright. Intent. Full of life and focused on her. He had laugh lines around those eyes, and his skin was lightly tanned, as if he spent some time outside. He had a strong jaw and a straight nose. A terrific, open face.

His body was nothing to sneeze at, either. Eve did a lightning-fast inventory, the quickest of once-overs. Broad, muscular shoulders, a trim waist, long, strong legs. She even liked the way he moved, the way he'd crossed the room to stand next to her. He seemed comfortable in his body, and not overly impressed with himself. Though he certainly had reason to be.

When she glanced at his mouth, naughty thoughts invaded her mind and she blushed, then took a quick sip of her rum punch. She felt so awkward. She just didn't know what she was doing. Having had all of two serious relationships in her life, Eve didn't consider herself terribly experienced or sophisticated—let alone, at ease—with the opposite sex.

He rescued the moment. "Max," he said, holding out his hand.

"Eve," she said, offering hers.

Touching this man constituted a small moment of ecstasy. She couldn't believe the effect one hand could have on another. He held hers a little longer than necessary, then released it. Not a sleazy move—just a gesture to let her know he was interested.

"So, what are you doing here?" he asked.

"The storm. It was pretty nasty out there."

"I know. I got here this morning, and was out taking a walk when the worst of it hit."

"It's so strange, so beautiful and so deadly. I was thinking about the birds and the squirrels out there in the cold, and was so glad to see that someone thought to put food out for them."

He fell in love. That instant. Hard. That this wonderful, beautiful, incandescent woman should care about a bunch of anonymous squirrels put her squarely over the top. He'd been dating—dating a *lot*—and the women he'd been spending time with weren't really concerned with anyone but themselves.

He liked this Eve. Correction. He adored her.

It didn't confound him, this instant emotion. His whole family, to hear Aunt Martha tell it, was pretty weird in one way or another, but especially when it came to love. His father had met his mother at a picnic, and that had been it for him. Now he'd met Eve over Christmas, at a bed and breakfast.

It would be a wonderful story to tell their children.

"And you?" she asked.

He couldn't follow her train of logic, and it must have shown in his expression.

"Where were you headed? Do you have family in the area?"

He smiled. "No. I just took a job here. My family is all in England at the moment. My father's a scientist—they packed up and moved over about three years ago."

They talked about England, about Stonehenge and Canterbury Cathedral, about scones and clotted cream, about Cornwall and London's best pubs. Then a woman with a broad, beaming face came into the parlor and announced that Christmas Eve dinner was served.

And what a dinner it was. Eve couldn't believe the amount of food, or how good it felt to sit at a table with almost twenty other people. The dining room was enormous, the table set with fine china, crystal and silver. The only light came from masses of candles on the table, and that served to make the entire experience terribly romantic in Eve's eyes.

Christmas Eve dinner was served family-style, and Max stayed right by her side. They stuffed themselves with roast turkey, dressing redolent with sage, mashed potatoes and gravy, candied yams, green beans, homemade cranberry chutney.... Then on to cakes and pies and tarts.

At the very end of the meal, over hot coffee, the inn's owners, the elderly man and his wife, proposed a toast.

"To all that we hold dear this holiday season," said the snowy-haired man, "dear God, let us give thanks and rejoice in the goodness of life."

And Eve, who felt as if she'd received a special blessing today, couldn't stop herself from smiling. She turned toward Max and caught her breath at the look in his eyes.

She almost couldn't look away. She did. She glanced back. He smiled. Slowly. Her lower lip trembled and she bit it to stop its movement.

He took hold of her hand beneath the table and she waited for the inevitable sexual move, for him to place it on his thigh. But he simply held her hand, linked their fingers together. His palm felt warm against hers. Right.

She looked down at her plate and blushed.

Sitting by the enormous Victorian Christmas tree in the front living room, they continued to talk long after the other guests had gone up to bed. The tree was gorgeous, covered with delicate pink rosebuds, Queen Anne's lace and tiny white lights.

Max coerced the bartender into giving them two glasses of some fine old brandy, and they sipped it slowly as they stared at the flames in the big front fireplace. And Eve thought of that solitary glass of wine she'd planned on having at home. This was infinitely better.

She wondered if she'd ever see Max again after this night, and found herself hoping she would.

"What about your parents?" she heard him say. He was leaning back on his side of the couch, studying her. She felt relaxed with him—yet excited at the same time—in a way she'd never felt with any other man.

What about your parents....

Perhaps it was meeting Max. Or the camaraderie of dinner, where her recent feelings of loneliness hadn't surfaced. Or maybe it was just the aftereffects of the brandy. But Eve found she couldn't quickly gloss over or suppress her emotions. Tears welled up in her eyes and she self-consciously turned her head away from him.

"Eve?" His voice was low and soft and, oh, so very tender.

She held up her hand toward him, palm out, as if holding him off while she tried to compose herself.

"Eve? Let me help you."

What wonderful words. She felt a handkerchief being pressed into her hand, and dabbed at her eyes. The tears were running over now, and she didn't protest as Max eased her gently down against him. Her cheek was against his shirtfront, she could feel the steady beating of his heart.

"My mother," she whispered. "She's ... gone."

He simply sat with her, stroked her hair.

"Christmas is . . . really hard."

"I know," he whispered.

"I miss her so much, and I feel so guilty because for a short while tonight I . . . I forgot. . . ."

"Shh." He kissed the top of her head. "I'm sure she wouldn't want you to feel guilty."

"No." She hiccuped on a sob, then blew her nose into his handkerchief.

"It's so hard to lose someone you love," he said.

She nodded her head.

"My sister lost her first child," he said quietly, still stroking her hair. "Right around Thanksgiving. It was literally years before we could all get together as a family again and celebrate."

"How awful."

"It was hardest on Annie. It took her a long time to come out of it. Deep depression. Sometimes, at quiet moments, I still see it in her eyes."

"Is she your older or younger sister?"

She heard the smile in his voice. "My twin."

She struggled up from the depths of the couch. His chest was too comfortable, his arms too inviting. Things were progressing way too fast, but until that moment it hadn't disturbed her. Now she felt too vulnerable. She really didn't know what she was doing, and wished for one desperate moment she had more knowledge of the intricacies of the mating ritual.

She could teach human sexuality at the university level, but real life was where she had a problem.

"Max."

"Yes?"

"I'm pretty tired."

"It's been a long day."

"I think . . . I think I want to turn in."

A blatant retreat on her part. Eve felt like Cinderella at the ball. She'd had her fun, but now it was time to retreat back inside herself, back to the old Eve. Back to safety.

"All right."

They got up off the couch and headed up the stairs. The fire had burned down to embers, but Max checked it carefully before they left, adjusting the screen. Now, as they mounted the stairs to the second floor, he stayed by her side as she approached her room.

How was she possibly going to make this man understand what his presence had meant to her? That he'd saved her holiday from being a day of despair and had given her a glimpse of what her life might someday be?

She stopped in front of her door, feeling utterly exhausted. She fumbled with her room key, and he gently took it out of her hand and opened the door. Her room looked cozy and inviting, a little island of serenity.

He handed her the key.

She couldn't seem to move inside the door.

She cleared her throat and was surprised to find she was trembling.

"Max? Thank you. I had . . . a wonderful time."

"Eve?"

She was looking up at his face; she couldn't seem to break eye contact with those beautiful blue eyes.

"Yes?"

"Can I kiss you good night?"

She hesitated. He saw it. A little of that light died in his eyes. Eve couldn't bear the thought that she had possibly hurt his feelings. Not her Max. Not this man she had come to—*like* so much in the short time they'd spent together.

She nervously wet her lips with the tip of her tongue.

He noticed.

"Yes."

He stepped forward, took her face in his hands. Eve swayed toward him, feeling the most incredible sense of surrender and inevitability.

He lowered his head and—

The door across the way opened. An enormous, muscle-bound man stepped outside with a tiny, fluffy white dog on a leash beside him.

"—and make sure Ginger does her business completely. I don't want her jumping up on the bed and waking me up at four in the morning!" The woman's voice sounded totally exasperated, and the man gave the two of them an embarrassed smile before he shut the door. He and the unfortunate Ginger trotted off down the carpeted hall.

Eve stared at Max, then put her hand over her mouth to stifle a laugh. Without thinking, she took his arm and pulled him into the dark bedroom, where, after she shut the door behind them, they both doubled over with laughter.

"Poor Ginger!" she gasped, wiping tears of laughter from her eyes. She approached the bedside lamp and turned it on, flooding the room with soft, intimate light. "With an owner like that, I'm surprised the poor little dog even jumps on the bed!"

Their laughter broke the tension. Max remarked that it was rather cold in the room, and knelt down to light the fire. The logs and kindling caught quickly. The light and warmth from the flames filled the room.

"Well," Max said quietly. "I'd better be going."

At that moment, Eve decided she didn't want to be a coward anymore. She was so tired of playing it safe. It had been a long time since her last relationship, and she suddenly realized how hungry she was for simple human contact.

Though she felt totally inexperienced, the most deeply feminine part of her yearned to be close to Max. A touch. A kiss. His scent. His skin. All her emotions and thoughts were focusing on one simple, human yearning. For that special feeling, that closeness that only a man could bring into her life.

And it had been a long time since she'd met a man as attractive as Max, as—*thrilling*, and she suddenly wanted to see where things could go.

If she let them.

"Max," she said softly, coming up behind him. He'd already started toward the door, obviously intent on leaving. "Max, don't go."

He turned and looked at her, his concentration complete. Everything stilled within her, and a wonderful, heart-stopping tension filled the room. He no longer looked like the successful professional man. Now there was something much more elemental, even slightly dangerous, in the way he was assessing her.

Silence. Then he said, so softly, "Whatever you want, Eve."

Just like that.

Her heart was racing inside her chest; she was sure he could hear it. He wanted her. She could sense it, she knew it. She had suspected it earlier, but here in the bedroom, the two of them alone, he didn't have to dilute his feelings. He didn't have to put on any sort of proper, social mask for the people downstairs.

They were alone.

"Do you want me to stay, Eve?"

She hesitated. Eve wasn't sure she wanted things to go this far, this fast. But she wanted him to stay. Just for a little bit.

"I want . . . I want you to kiss me."

He smiled at her again—that slow, sexy smile. That smile she wanted to believe was hers alone. Then he moved, slowly, steadily, until he was standing in front of her, his hands on her shoulders, his fingers moving in little, soothing circles on her upper arms. She sensed he wasn't totally aware of the way he was touching her, and that made his actions even more exciting.

"Eve," he said, his voice low. Raspy. Sexy, with a wealth of emotion just in the way he said her name. It thrilled her; she felt it down to the tips of her toes. "Eve."

Her throat was so tight, she could barely breathe. She looked up at him, pressed her palms against his broad shoulders, leaned against him as his strong hands framed her face, as that beautiful mouth lowered over hers.

Their lips met.

Kismet. Fate. Her heartbeat sped up, she couldn't seem to think, and her last conscious thought was that they were both lost. . . .

2

LUST WASN'T EXACTLY the right word. On fire. Crazed. Two passionate beings with no thought but the fulfillment of the moment. When Max kissed her, she simply went to a different place. Everything she'd ever thought about the dangers and inadvisability of a one-night stand—nothing seemed to matter anymore.

Nothing mattered but getting closer to him. Getting his jacket and shirt off. Seeing that muscled expanse of chest covered with dark hair, feeling that rapid heartbeat beneath the palm of her hand. The warmth of his skin, the beat of his heart, the press of his lips on hers—

She couldn't think, could only feel.

His lips covered hers, tasted, teased, caressed. She couldn't stop where the two of them were headed; there was the most delicious, passionate feeling of inevitability. This was going to happen. She wanted it to happen. They had been building up to this moment with each glance, each word.

Their foreplay had all taken place downstairs.

She made no sound of protest when his hand found the zipper at the back of her dress. He slid it down, not gently, but with the roughness of genuine, raw need.

The back of the dress fell away from her skin; then he was touching her bare back.

She wanted more. His jacket was off, and his shirt was already half off, her hands skimming over the muscles of his chest, moving lower, caressing the hardness of his abdomen.

He groaned. She smiled. Nothing about this day had been ordinary, and she had the feeling she was in for the night of her life.

He was aggressive, and she loved it. He kissed her mouth, her throat, down to where the dress fell away slightly. He pulled it farther down, then unfastened the front catch of her bra. Her breasts were bare, then covered with his hands, his mouth.

She couldn't be shy with him now. She couldn't even think; her brain seemed to refuse to work. Shyness, inexperience, trepidation—none of it mattered against the onslaught of sensual feelings. It was as if her body had taken over, with its deep wisdom overriding any doubts or fears her mind might have had.

Eve moaned, her head falling back. His large hand was warm on her back, supporting her, holding her, capturing her. She couldn't move away, couldn't protest what he was doing to her—didn't want to.

He took her hand in his, then brought it to the front of his jeans and pressed it against the hard ridge of his arousal. Pressed it there, kept it there. Touching him this intimately was an unbelievable turn-on.

He maneuvered her toward the bed, and she felt her legs press against the mattress. Then she was tumbling backward, bouncing slightly on the bed. His hands were already at the hem of her velvet dress, sliding it swiftly, determinedly up her thighs. He paused for a fraction of a second when he discovered the stockings and garter belt, then ripped the thin silken barrier of her panties out of the way.

That got her going like nothing else. No man on earth had ever ripped underwear off her in his haste, and she was astonished to find out she liked it.

A lot.

He'd kicked off his boots; now he was unfastening his jeans. Bracing herself on her elbows, she watched him. There was something so masculine, so determined, so sexy about a man stripping off his clothes with one thing on his mind.

Then he covered her, slid between her thighs. She felt him press himself against her, hard and hot and full, ready. More than ready. Then he was inside her, filling, stretching, giving her so much pleasure that her head fell back and she heard soft, breathy moans coming from her mouth, sounds she couldn't control. She, who had never made a sound in her life, whose brief experiences with sex had been overwhelmingly careful, polite, proper, didn't know what to do with this wild storm they were creating.

He grabbed her buttocks, pulled her toward him, sank even deeper. She caught her breath. Then he was kissing her, moving inside her, making her come alive and feel sensual, sexual feelings she'd never even been aware she possessed. In some ways, climaxing had always been a bit of a chore for her; she'd dreaded hearing that inevitable masculine question, giving the reassurance men always seemed to need.

Now her response was so wild, so unfettered, it almost embarrassed her. But her brain seemed to have no room for fear or shame or apprehension. She could only feel his hard arousal inside her, feel his hot, sure hands moving restlessly over her skin, feel his fingers biting into her hips as he pushed farther, touching her as deeply as possible—

He cut her scream off with a kiss as she climaxed, the contractions almost wrenched from her, from the deepest place inside her. His sexual tempo increased, became impossibly fast; then he was slamming into her and finding his own release. She kissed him, held on to him, never wanted to let him go.... Never...

Then the room was silent except for their breathing and the sounds of the fire. Eve kept her eyes closed, almost afraid of what she would find when she opened them. She felt a kiss on her cheek, then on the corner of her lips.

He wasn't going to go away.

She opened her eyes. He was propped up on his forearms and smiling down at her. She let out a long, slow breath as she looked up at him. Then she took another, and let it out. Slowly.

What did one say at a moment like this?

He touched his forehead to hers and closed his eyes, and at that moment looked so touchingly, achingly vulnerable that her throat constricted.

"Ho, ho, ho," he whispered, then kissed her.

Laughter bubbled up, wonderful laughter, and the strange thing was that as she got the giggles all over again, she realized she'd never really laughed in bed with a man before. Not until now.

She couldn't stop it; the waves washed over her. He was still inside her, and she saw he was laughing, as well. With sheer, unadulterated masculine delight.

"Merry Christmas," she whispered, and then for some insane reason erupted into another gale of giggles.

"And what would you like in your stocking, little girl?" He was already hard again, and she felt him give a little twitch inside her. She caught her breath.

"Again?"

He looked disgustingly pleased with himself.

"You," he said, kissing the tip of her nose, "are ravishing. But we have a problem."

"We do?"

"You have too many clothes on."

She considered this. He was buck naked, while she had everything on but her ripped panties.

"Call me crazy," he whispered against her mouth just before he kissed her, "but I'd really like to see you naked."

"With the lights on?"

He frowned, clearly puzzled by her logic. "You're going to get modest now?"

Good point. "Um, I guess not."

"Good." When he moved off her, she sat up and shimmied out of her dress. Her unhooked bra met with the same fate. For once in her life she was thankful she'd splurged on some really wonderful lingerie. The push-up bra and garter belt were wisps of black lace and silk, the stockings sheer and sexy.

On a naughty little whim, and totally unlike her, Eve got up and walked across the room to hang up her dress, wearing only the garter belt, stockings and her black heels.

Max lay back in the canopied bed, watching her.

"This," he said softly, "is as good as it gets."

"Thank you." She walked back toward the bed. He'd turned off the bedside lamp—a thoughtful gesture toward her modesty—and now the room was bathed in soft, flickering firelight. Max lit one of the fat red candles on the bedside table, blew out the match, and the scent of cinnamon filled the air.

"What now?" she asked, sitting next to him. She knew, of course. It wasn't difficult to see how their evening was going to proceed. Ignoring an arousal as impressive as Max's was impossible.

"I'm wondering if you should leave the shoes on." He said this with such a delightful sense of fun, she couldn't help but smile.

"You're not one of those fetishists who hid in their mother's closets, are you?"

"Nah. I just like what heels do to your legs." He slid a large, warm hand up one of her stockinged thighs.

She shivered with reaction.

"What would you like?" he whispered.

She felt her face flame. No man had ever asked her that before. Come to think of it, she hadn't really ever done a lot of talking in bed.

"I . . . ah . . . don't know."

He took her hand and gently kissed the palm. "Come on. You must think it. Tell me. Down and dirty. Anything."

She hesitated.

He was grinning, not at her embarrassment, but with an infectious love of life. "Anything, Eve. Anything for you."

"Ohh." Her head fell back, and she lay down on the bed. "Would you just hold me for a moment?"

He obliged.

His warm skin felt wonderful against hers. But now, within this moment of relative calm, her mind started working again, wondering at her body's response, wondering at how this could have all happened to her. She wasn't this sort of woman. She didn't do this sort of thing.

"You seem nervous," he whispered, kissing the back of her neck. They lay like spoons, facing the fire.

"It's kind of difficult to . . . ignore that."

"That?"

She nudged her hips against his erection. "That."

"Ignore it? I thought we were planning what to do with it."

She covered her face with her hands and he laughed.

"I suppose," she whispered in an agony of sudden embarrassment, "that it's too late to say that—"

"I'm not that kind of a girl? Me, either. Boy, I mean." He turned her in his arms so she was facing him, their bellies pressed together, the evidence of his desire poking her gently. "I don't know how to tell you this," he whispered.

"What?" she asked, alarm welling up inside her.

"I feel so . . . cheap. So sordid, degraded. Used."

Relieved, she started to laugh again, and he hugged her close.

"Eve." He kissed her. "Eve." He kissed her again. She could feel herself melting into a wonderful, sexual, completely submissive state. She'd do anything, want anything, become anything for this man. She wanted to stay in this room forever, to never leave....

"Tell me," he whispered, gently biting her earlobe. "I want to make you happy."

"Oh well, okay, I can do this, I can—"

He silenced her with a quick, playful kiss. "Don't talk. Just feel. Then tell me whatever you want to do, whatever will make you feel good."

"I think I'd like—" She leaned over and whispered in his ear.

"We can do that." He rolled over on his back and pulled her up on top of him. His hands cupped and shaped her breasts, his fingertips teasing her nipples and making her moan. "You're so pretty," he whispered, and the genuine note of masculine wonder in his voice almost brought tears to her eyes.

Slowly, wanting this moment to last, she eased herself down on him, sighing with feminine pleasure as his rigid length filled her. Max was a generous man in every sense of the word.

"Are we doing okay?" she whispered. Eve felt so sexually unsophisticated. At thirty-three she'd only had two serious relationships in her life. She wasn't a woman who gave her heart easily, and had been devastated by each breakup. Which was why this whole evening was so remarkable.

His voice sounded a little strained. "We're doing a lot more than okay—" He reached for her hips to hold her still for a moment.

"Talk to me, Eve."

It was as if sensual floodgates opened. She knew she would never see this man again. She knew she'd never be able to look him in the eye if she did, after the night they'd spent and what they'd done.

And what they were about to do.

But for once in her life, she wanted to take something she wanted, just for herself. Eve wanted to feel alive. She wanted Max the way she'd never wanted any other man, despite the fact that she really didn't know him that well.

Sex with a stranger. A perfect, desirable stranger. A man who was making her come alive, out of the self-imposed deep freeze she'd put her feelings in for years. She was enough of a psychologist to know that, on a very primal, primitive level, this was good for her.

"I'd like to try—" She leaned down and whispered a sensual suggestion in his ear.

"Oh, yeah." He grinned up at her.

"You're sure?"

"With bells on."

She laughed. "And then maybe we could—" She felt her face flush as she leaned down and whispered another suggestion.

"I like your mind. Absolutely. I like that a lot."

"And perhaps we could finish with—" Another whisper, and this time those bright blue eyes really lit up.

"I'm game if you are."

"Max," she whispered as she slowly eased herself down until she was lying full length on top of him. She kissed him, delighting in his instantaneous response. For just this one night, he was hers. "My Max." She cupped his face gently in her hands, her thumbs rubbing his cheekbones, and kissed him again.

SNOWFLAKES TAPPED SOFTLY against the windows as Eve woke up. It took her a few moments to come to a full realization of where she was, what she'd done—

Who she'd done it with—

Oh my God.

She eased herself up on one elbow. Max slept the sleep of the truly exhausted, flat on his back, one of the down pillows over his head, his naked body partially concealed beneath the twisted, lacy mauve sheets.

Images of him flashed through Eve's mind—sensual, blatantly sexual, raw, tender and funny. All in one delightfully muscled package. With an impressive brain.

She glanced at his flat abdomen, its gentle rise and fall, the arrow of dark hair that trailed down beneath the sheets to—

She took a deep breath. Max was impressive in every respect.

Eve swung her legs over the side of the bed and sat for a moment, considering what to do. If she bolted and ran like the emotional coward she was, she could have this perfect memory for the rest of her life. If she stayed, Max could become another bad memory.

What if he'd only wanted a roll in the hay? After all, he hadn't promised her anything. He'd said he was moving on to a new job, and by implication, a new life. They were like the proverbial ships that passed in the night, and neither of them should try to make

more out of this chance encounter than it actually
was.

Which was great sex. Correction. *Phenomenal sex*.
Now she knew what all the fuss was about, why her
students were always so agitated. Now it all made
sense.

She rubbed her temples, sensing the beginnings of
a tension headache. What to do?

Okay. She was an adult woman of the nineties. She
could do this, she could carry this one-night stand to
its logical conclusion. She'd leave. She'd leave gracefully. She'd be out of this room so fast, he wouldn't
even know what hit him.

Piece of cake. Max slept soundly; the poor guy had
put in a hell of a lot of effort last night. She'd lost count
of the number of times they'd made love, then she'd
fallen asleep, happily exhausted, in his arms. She'd
tried out most of her sexiest fantasies, and Max had
suggested a few that had been so arousing, her toes
had curled.

All in all, a spectacular success.

But now she had to face the morning after.

Perhaps a note? No. What could she say? *Thank
you, Max, for saving me from myself. Thank you for
awakening me to my deepest needs. A part of me
would have remained dead if it hadn't been for you....*

There was so much she wished she could tell him.
But so much she was afraid he'd never understand.

She sat on the edge of the large bed, her emotions at war as she ran a hand through her mussed hair.

Go.

Stay.

Now.

No.

Stay and risk your heart. Lay it on the line, because something this wonderful comes along only once in a lifetime.

Eve bit her lip, in an agony of indecision.

Or you can run like the dirty dog you are, because if you find out Max only wanted you for one night, you'll be totally shattered.

Yes.

No.

She covered her face with her hands and sat.

Max stirred in his sleep. She froze, then her brain kicked into overdrive.

Go.

She got up off the bed, dressed swiftly in sweats and sneakers, crammed her velvet dress, lingerie and toiletries into her bag, then sneaked out of the room, closing the door softly behind her. She didn't even bother to take her elaborate goody bag. In her state of emotional agitation, she wouldn't have been able to choke down one gumdrop.

This time, she carried her own bag out to her car.

MAX SAT UP in bed when the door clicked shut. He ran his hand over his face, then shook his head slowly.

"Oh, Eve."

He'd suspected she was going to run. Sensed it. And so, operating under the infallible logic that all was fair in love and war, he'd done the one thing he'd had to do. He'd waited until she'd fallen asleep and taken a peek inside her purse. Her wallet, to be precise. Just to get an address, a way to locate her.

Because this relationship, though it had literally started out with a bang, was far from over.

What he'd found had astonished him. Delighted him. As a scientist, he worked with the ways of the universe to find order out of chaos. Though the chaos theory had caught fire in intellectual circles, now the new physics was proving there was an order to the universe that, up until now, had not even been suspected.

Max had long known this, on an instinctual and spiritual level. In layman's terms, it boiled down to "things often work out for the best for all concerned."

She wouldn't be able to get away from him. He'd have all the time in the world for his courtship of her. Because the new job he'd accepted, that started directly after the first of the year, was at none other than Middleton University.

EVE LET HERSELF into her silent, dark house. The birches outside seemed to mock her. No candlelight, no warmth, no wreaths, no twinkling Christmas trees here. No scented potpourri or fragrant gingerbread. All the presents she had were in the trunk of her Volvo.

It was just as well. Anything to do with Christmas would have only made her miss Max more than she already did.

She flung down her suitcase, gave Caliban a hug and a kiss, then called Gail to let her know where she was. After pouring herself that promised glass of wine, she took the longest bubble bath on record, then climbed into bed.

From her safe haven beneath the covers, she attempted to come to terms with what had happened. How could she have totally thrown off all traces of herself and become someone else? How could she have deviated so completely from that safe little life plan she had all mapped out?

It wasn't like her.

But, damn it, it had felt *right*.

Now she felt awful about leaving Max. Tears came to her eyes as she remembered him.

I feel so . . . cheap. So sordid, degraded. Used.

She laughed through her tears, then punched her pillow and sobbed. Because the truth was, she was a coward. She'd had a chance at happiness with a wonderful man, a chance at starting something special, and fear had caused her to run for her life.

"Sometimes," she whispered to a contented Caliban, curled up on the pillow beside her, "I disgust even myself."

MAX DECIDED TO REMAIN at Swan's Bed and Breakfast for a few more days. Originally he'd been planning to arrive at the university early. But now he had a battle plan to put into effect, so he thought it prudent to stay out of sight until the big New Year's Eve party the faculty head, Dr. Crummond, was throwing to announce his arrival.

He missed Eve. Romantic soul that he was, he'd asked to be moved from his original room to the one they'd shared. He'd also bought a small crystal swan from the gift shop, thinking of Eve the entire time. Wondering what she was doing.

He lay on the comfortable bed in this room that was full of erotic memories and daydreamed about her. Max thought of what would happen when they met again. And he smiled as he heard his large, long-haired tabby cat, Kevin, grumbling from beneath the bed. Kevin was not a happy traveler, and this vacation was no exception.

Christmas Day would be a lot more fun if Eve had chosen to stay. Max wasn't looking forward to the elaborate dinner without her by his side.

But Max thought he might have an inkling of why she'd run. He remembered their conversation in the front room about her mother. She needed a little time.

He didn't, but then he was sure where he was going, and where he wanted this relationship to end up. He could afford to be patient.

But once he arrived on campus, it would be all or nothing. He'd chosen to lose this battle, but he planned on winning the war.

THE PHONE RANG, its sound a shrill awakening. Eve groped for the receiver, her head still beneath the covers.

"H'lo?" She cleared her throat. "Hello?"

"Eve? Patty. I saw your car in the driveway and I thought, if you didn't have any other plans, would you like to join Glen and I for Christmas dinner?"

Glen and Patty Dalton. He was another professor in the psychology department, she the ultimate faculty wife. They'd had no children during the course of their twelve-year marriage, and were extraordinarily close. Eve was fond of both of them, and dinner with the Daltons sounded just right.

"It sounds wonderful, Patty. I'd love to. What time?"

"Fiveish?"

"I'll be there."

Patty laughed, and Eve could picture her short blond bob, her delicate face. "Actually, there was an ulterior motive to my asking."

"Uh-oh."

"I don't want Glen to have to face Dr. Crummond alone."

This brought Eve to an upright sitting position in bed. "Crummond the curmudgeon is coming to Christmas dinner? Can I take a rain check on your invite?"

"Oh, please, Eve, you've got to come. I'm looking forward to this dinner like I look forward to a root canal."

Eve paused, considering.

"Do you have a present for him under your tree?"

"A book."

"Can you put my name on the card?"

"Sure."

Eve sighed. "All right. For you and Glen."

"Thanks, Eve. Crummond's all jazzed up about that new guy who's joining the faculty."

"Dr. Alexander Elliott. He gave me an article about him. He's awfully young to have accomplished as much as he has. He'll make Glen and I look like real slackers."

Patty laughed. "What did he look like?"

"There wasn't a picture."

"Probably your typical bookish type. A real nerd. Crummond's just in love with him. He's over the moon that Middleton got him."

Eve sighed. "I know. Now, with the curmudgeon coming, I can't show up in sweats. What are you wearing?"

"A long plaid skirt and that black top."

"Okay. That gives me a jumping-off point."

"Drinks at four."

"Patty?"

"Yeah?"

"Don't push your luck."

"MIDDLETON IS DAMN LUCKY to have been able to attract a man of Elliott's caliber." Dr. Crummond cut a slice of his ham, then chewed decisively. Eve thought to herself, not for the first time, that the elderly department head looked like a gigantic toad.

"Patty, this Cumberland sauce is superb, if I do say so myself." Dr. Crummond beamed. A happy toad, Eve silently amended.

"Thank you." Patty chanced a look at her husband. Normally, Glen Dalton was the most easygoing of men, strolling around campus in well-worn jeans, boots and flannel shirts. She'd always thought he looked like a lumberjack. His height, his bright red hair and full beard made him stand out. Now he seemed anxious.

"The two of you," Dr. Crummond said, eyeing both Glen and Eve, "are part of the younger faculty. Not so stuffy and set in your ways. I want you both to promise me that you'll go out of your way to welcome Dr. Elliott to Middleton. Make him feel at home. I'd very much like for him to stay on longer than just the one semester."

"Is he still going to do that series of lectures?" Eve asked.

"Yes. You'll all be expected to attend, of course."

"Of course," Glen and Eve said in unison.

"I'm intrigued by the Cyber Baby," Patty said, and Eve gave her a slight nod, indicating she knew how her friend was trying to direct the conversation toward subjects that would keep Dr. Crummond in a good mood. Patty's delicate face seemed to glow with animation tonight, perhaps with the effort of being the perfect hostess.

"Brilliant invention. But then, I'm not surprised. Elliott's father is a scientist, as well. He probably learned from a master."

Patty warmed to her subject, now that she knew she had Dr. Crummond's approval. "The idea of creating a doll that would show young men and women the real responsibilities of raising a child. I really admire him for thinking of that. When I was in Home Ec, we had a child-care class, but we used five-pound sacks of flour as our babies."

"We used eggs," Eve said.

"The Cyber Baby revolutionized all that," Dr. Crummond said, cutting another piece of ham. "Once that key is turned on, for all intents and purposes, that robotic doll is as close to a real baby as it's possible to invent."

"Didn't he have a sister?" Glen added. "Wasn't she the reason he invented the Cyber Baby?"

The article Eve had read had already given her the answer to this question, but she wisely let Dr. Crummond have the floor.

"Yes. She got pregnant at a very young age. Lost the child. Stillborn." Dr. Crummond cleared his throat. "Terrible tragedy. Terrible. It affected young Elliott deeply. He said he never wanted another woman to have to go through the pain his sister had. Hence, the Cyber Baby."

Eve thought of her previous evening with Max, and how his twin had also lost a child. She found reasons to think about him constantly, but now forced herself to stay in the present. With Dr. Crummond at the table, she had to keep her wits about her.

"Will he be bringing one of his robotic dolls with him?" Patty asked.

Dr. Crummond finished chewing the last of his ham, swallowed, then sat back in his chair, totally content.

"Not only is he bringing one with him, he's going to be working on a new, improved model."

"Fascinating," Eve said, and meant it.

A hazelnut torte and espresso were served, the presents were opened—Dr. Crummond loved his book. Finally, Eve was just about to leave when he made one last announcement.

"Now, the three of you will be at my New Year's party to welcome Dr. Elliott, won't you?"

"Wouldn't miss it," Glen replied smoothly, and Eve caught the look that passed between him and Patty.

"Like I said before, I want you all to work hard to make this man feel welcome."

"We will," Eve said. She was fascinated by the fact that Dr. Crummond seemed both genuinely in awe of this man and a little intimidated by him.

Dr. Crummond scratched his chin thoughtfully. "Bit of an eccentric, or so I've been told. Most real geniuses are. He may dress in a rather strange fashion, or make bizarre statements from time to time. I want you all to go with the flow, as you young people say. Whatever Elliott says is right. Make him feel at ease, as if Middleton is his home. I want this matter to take precedence over everything else. Just be sure your classes don't slide."

Eve, Glen and Patty nodded obediently.

NEW YEAR'S. A night Eve usually dreaded.

But tonight wouldn't be so bad. At least she had a party to go to. Dr. Crummond was a widower, his wife having died six years ago. But he'd always entertained in style, hiring the best caterers. Held in the huge old house up on the hill overlooking the college, his parties were always major campus events.

Tonight, as anxious as he was to impress Dr. Alexander Elliott, he would undoubtedly pull out all the stops.

She had a great dress to wear, more risqué than the clothing she usually bought. Since her wild night with Max, Eve had been consciously reassessing her life. She'd thought of Max constantly since she'd chickened out and left him lying in bed, and had finally decided she'd liked the final effect he'd had on her.

Eve had come to the conclusion that she wanted to be a little more daring, to try to put a small element of adventure into her life. Excitement. Pizzazz. One could only live a careful, cloistered existence for so long. Max had taught her the folly of living that way.

He'd helped her out of her sometimes-paralyzing shyness that night at the inn. It had only been possible, of course, because she'd been so absolutely sure she'd never, ever see him again. Therefore she'd been able to cut loose and act out all the fantasies that had been deep within her mind all these years. She owed him a genuine debt, and was thankful, but knew she'd never see him again.

A part of her liked that. After all, that was the true definition of a one-night stand.

The dress she had for tonight's party was black lace shot through with gold metallic thread, sexy without being too provocative. This was a small campus, after all, and people would talk if she wore anything too outrageous.

She tried styling her hair into an elegant upsweep, then gave up and let it settle around her shoulders, wild and free. It had just enough curl to be stubborn, though it didn't frizz. Eve put on a little more eye makeup than usual, then slipped into high heels and walked downstairs to wait for Glen and Patty to pick her up. They'd decided on safety in numbers, and had also planned to have coffee afterward and dissect the renowned Dr. Elliott.

They arrived right on time, striving neither to make an anxious early entrance or come fashionably late. Dr. Crummond answered the door himself. This time, Eve thought, he looked like a very flushed and slightly bombed little toad.

"Come in, come in!" He gave Glen a hearty slap on his broad shoulders that almost sent him reeling. "I can't wait for you to meet our new faculty member. Elliott has just been regaling me with his stories. Quite brilliant, you know."

Eve gave a young student her coat, then followed Dr. Crummond into his enormous living room, packed with faculty members.

A man was standing facing the fire. The famous Dr. Elliott, no doubt. He struck her as something of a maverick when it came to dress, certainly not conservative, for he wore a pair of black Levi's, black boots and a black sweater. His brown hair gleamed in the firelight, his shoulders were broad, his legs long and muscular. There was something familiar, too familiar—

Eve felt her heart begin to speed up.

No . . .

"Oh, my!" Patty whispered under her breath.

"Elliott!" Dr. Crummond called. "I'd like you to meet two more of our faculty members, Glen Dalton and Eve Vaughn—"

Eve didn't hear any more. Couldn't. The man in black turned. Smiled. He sported just a hint of stubble on his cheeks and chin, and it only served to make him seem even more dangerous. Lethal. The look he sent her would have melted the ice on the sidewalk outside.

Time stopped. A peculiar roaring sound filled her ears. For a moment, she thought she might faint. Her heart pounded, her blood raced, her cheeks flamed so bright and hot, she could've sworn she was burning up with fever.

Max!

3

"DR. VAUGHN," Max said, extending a hand.

Eve felt a relief almost palpable in its intensity. He wasn't going to blow her cover. He wasn't going to make any reference at all to that wild, sensual, totally-out-of-character-for-her Christmas Eve they'd spent at the bed and breakfast.

Max was going to be a gentleman.

"Dr. Elliott," she said, grasping that hand, that lifeline he extended toward her. She shook it, trying very hard not to let him see how his touch affected her, furiously blocking out memories of exactly what that hand had done to her....

Further introductions were made, and Glen and Patty welcomed Max to the university. Dr. Crummond beamed. Eve thought about heading to the bathroom and spending the rest of what promised to be an intolerably long evening hidden away. Or perhaps she could escape to Dr. Crummond's extensive library on the second floor.

Immature? Yes. Comforting? Absolutely.

Max simply overwhelmed her. What they'd had was supposed to be over. Those were the basic rules of a one-night stand. You could be wild and crazy because you knew you would never, ever see that person again in your lifetime. It was supposed to be a sensual moment out of time.

If she'd had any idea he was going to show up at Middleton, she never would have asked him into her room that night—

Oh yes, you would have, a tiny voice inside her whispered.

You're right. I wouldn't have missed it for the world, she answered herself back.

"God, he's gorgeous," Patty whispered as the two of them moved toward the buffet line. "He looks like the actor in that movie—"

"George Clooney," Eve said, finally remembering the actor's name. Those vivid eyes, that slight stubble, that sexy-as-sin sandpaper voice, that bedside manner—

Oh, God. This was going to be one tough evening.

"He makes me wish," Patty continued whispering as they reached one end of the buffet table, "that I was single again. And that's saying a lot, 'cause I love Glen to pieces and it would take a hell of a man to make me even *think* that way." She sighed. "But I can fantasize—"

"Let's eat," Eve said abruptly, taking her friend's arm and steering her toward the plates and silverware, then the platters piled high with food and drink. Someone—some caterer—had prepared a feast worthy of Martha Stewart. Not unlike Swan's Bed and

Breakfast. Normally she would have enjoyed this part of the evening, but now her stomach felt as if she were poised on the top of a roller coaster. Ready for a plummeting drop.

Dr. Crummond had gone all out. Swedish meatballs, a huge turkey, caviar, breads and cheeses, a vegetable casserole, winter apples and pears, gilded nuts, a huge punch bowl filled with wassail, candies and cookies and pies, holiday fudge—

"Looks good, doesn't it?" She heard that voice, then turned, plate in hand, to see Max by her side.

A noise came out of Patty's mouth that sounded suspiciously like a whimper. Eve aimed a delicate, unobtrusive kick in the direction of her friend's ankle.

"The department head's going all out for you, Dr. Elliott," Eve replied, trying to keep her tone calm. Bland. "We all want you to feel welcome." Her voice wasn't trembling, and she was thankful because almost every other part of her body was. Eve tried desperately to stop the turmoil inside that threatened to tear her apart. She hadn't known how badly she wanted to see Max again until he was here, standing in front of her.

"Call me Max."

She hesitated. "Max."

His eyes were kind. He wasn't toying with her, but he was stating his intentions. Making them perfectly clear. This was a male animal clearly in pursuit.

A part of her was thrilled. Just as a part of her was terrified. She found herself in a frustratingly ambivalent state of mind. Why couldn't she have met Max at a different time of her life, when she had a little more confidence in her skills with the opposite sex? Why did she have to feel so . . . *inept,* for lack of a better word.

You think too much, Eve. But then again, maybe you should. Look where feeling got you—

"May I call you Eve?"

She blinked and thought of the myriad ways he'd seen her that night: dressed, undressed, partially dressed. Strutting in front of him clad only in a garter belt and stockings. In bed, her head back, eyes closed, totally lost in ecstasy. Screaming at that crucial moment, until he covered her mouth with his own.

The thought of being formal with him struck her as ludicrous.

"All right."

"So, what are you ladies going to have?" Max turned his attention back to the food-laden table as Patty whimpered again, another tiny little squeak. Eve glared at her, then turned back to Max.

"I already ate. Perhaps just one of these desserts, and then . . ." *Then I can make a quick getaway. Exit, stage right. Think things over. Ponder what to do. . . .*

In her mind, Max's appearance negated the need to follow social convention.

"But I thought you didn't eat dinner," Patty began, loading her plate. Eve closed her eyes, felt her face flush and wished the floor would open up and swallow her. Patty moved ahead, joining her husband at the other end of the large buffet table, and Eve found herself alone with Max.

He lowered his voice so she was the only one who could hear him. "Are you nervous?"

She didn't know what to do. It was impossible to try for sophistication. Eve nodded her head.

"Don't be. It's going to be okay."

Easy for you to say.

She jumped when Dr. Crummond came up behind her and placed a hand on her shoulder.

"I'm delighted to see the two of you are getting on so well!" His voice boomed out. Eve surmised he was nervous and had indulged in his infamous wassail to calm his nerves. Usually the department head was a lot more formal.

Dr. Crummond lowered his voice and whispered, for Eve's ears alone, "Remember what I said. You and Glen—be nice."

How much nicer can I be? I've already slept with him.

A glimpse of a smile played on Max's face as he watched her. The expression touched his lips briefly, then he seemed to force a bland look on his face. But his eyes sparkled. Danced with emotion. Not at her expense. He seemed genuinely delighted to see her again.

Eve took a deep breath. She should try to be more courageous when it came to matters of the heart. With a look like that in his eyes, what could she lose? She smiled back at him, then proceeded to move along down the lavish buffet.

She filled her plate in a haphazard fashion, then headed toward a group of seats by a large bay window. She joined Glen and Patty there, balancing her plate in her lap and wishing she hadn't chosen this night to wear such a sexy evening dress.

Max joined them, totally at ease.

Eve speared a meatball, popped it into her mouth and chewed automatically. It could have come out of a can of dog food for all the attention she gave it.

Max started an easy conversation with Glen about the psychology department, and Eve took the opportunity to study him. He seemed so at ease, so genuinely interested in everything Glen had to say. When Max laughed, she couldn't resist smiling. He really was a charming man, and she began to understand why she'd fallen prey to that insane impulse, that one-night stand.

Who wouldn't have?

Okay. Calm down. He was your Christmas present to yourself, right? And now he's here, and it doesn't mean anything, and it doesn't mean you have to start anything up again, it simply means...that you want to.

She almost choked on a piece of broccoli.

She did want to. Badly. Somehow, in a totally inexplicable way, Eve couldn't look at this man and not think about sex. Maybe it was that deep, scratchy, bedroom voice. Maybe it was those dark blue eyes. Maybe it was what those hands were capable of. That incredible body. *Or maybe it was the fact that he ripped off my underwear and made me scream with ecstasy—*

"Eve?"

"What?" Everyone in the small group was looking at her. She realized she had tuned out again. Eve told herself to stop letting her thoughts run astray and deal with the present moment.

"Your specialty is in human sexuality?" Max asked.

Yeah, right. Except in my own life. She opened her mouth. Closed it. Whipped her composure around herself and said, "Yes."

Glen nodded. "You'll have to attend one of her classes. She's teaching an advanced seminar this semester."

The thought of Max in her classroom made her heart skip a beat. Though she was a mature woman and could talk knowledgeably about any aspect of the human body and sexuality, she knew she couldn't possibly keep her cool with Max in the audience.

"I look forward to that." He gave her a bland smile and she fought the urge to kick him.

Out of the corner of her eye Eve saw Dr. Crummond approaching their group and she knew she had to say something. Quickly.

"You're giving a series of lectures yourself, aren't you?"

"Yes."

"On?"

"The sociobiology of love." He grinned. "And sex."

"That'll be a crowd pleaser on this campus," Glen said, earning a quick laugh from Patty. "Be sure to make the posters look X-rated."

"It's fascinating stuff, this mating dance of ours," Max said conversationally. Eve was thankful he hadn't singled her out. He really was being quite the gentleman. "There's a definite order to courtship, and all of it makes perfect sense. It's when we get the order mixed up, or skip steps, that we sometimes get ourselves into trouble."

Glen nodded again. "Like the way we all were in high school. A definite order. First base, second base—"

"Oh, brother, these sports analogies," Patty said. But she was smiling fondly at her husband.

"Third base, and a home run," Max finished. Both men laughed. "But there's a reason for those steps. A reason we interact the way we do. That's the kind of information I'll be covering."

"Hmm." Now Patty seemed intrigued. Eve simply glanced down at her plate and speared another meatball.

"Do you teach?" Max asked Patty.

"Nope. I run the coffeehouse on Main Street. But to get back to what you were talking about, what happens when a man and woman skip those steps? I mean, Glen and I met in college, so we had a pretty traditional courtship—"

"Not that I didn't want things to progress a little faster," Glen interrupted.

Eve decided that the only way to make this evening bearable was to follow Dr. Crummond's example. She took a large swallow of spiced ale.

Patty gave her husband a playful punch on the arm. "No, seriously. This is intriguing stuff. What if, say, a man and a woman met, and maybe had a one-night stand—"

The wassail went down the wrong way. Before she could stop her reaction, Eve snapped forward as her drink exploded back up, through her nose, all over her plate and the front of her dress.

Max came to the rescue.

He took her plate off her lap, then pulled her to her feet. Still coughing furiously, she felt him briskly raise her arms, then thump her back. Despite the distractions, her body still responded to his closeness.

"Everything all right over here?" she heard Dr. Crummond say above the roaring in her ears.

"Could we get some privacy?" Max said.

"Certainly."

She didn't know why, but her legs didn't want to work. Eve knew she hadn't drank that much wassail. It had to be the shock; Max had simply overwhelmed her, taken over her senses. She clutched the front of his black sweater, then looked up at him, feeling panicky. He frowned when he saw the expression in her eyes.

"Come with me," he said. Then before she could make a protest, he swung her up into his arms.

THE LIBRARY OFFERED sanctuary. Eve could hear the muted sounds of the party downstairs, but it was quiet and warm up here, among the book-lined walls. One of the students had brought them each another plate of food, and now Eve found herself lying on a comfortable couch covered in bloodred velvet.

The entire room was old-fashioned, like a library from a century ago. Heavy furniture, dark wood. Books everywhere. A Tiffany lamp. A few little knickknacks.

And, of course, Max.

"How are you feeling?"

She pushed her hair out of her eyes, tried to sit up.

"Just lie there for a little. You were choking pretty badly."

She lay back. It was oddly comforting, letting him take care of her.

"I'm sorry. I just . . ."

"I know. What Patty said got to you."

She nodded her head.

"It wasn't supposed to happen this way," she began.

He simply listened, and she knew he would give her all the time in the world to tell him what she was feeling. If only she could explain it in some sort of coherent fashion.

"It was supposed to be . . ." She hesitated.

"An isolated moment out of time," he finished for her, after a long pause.

"Yes."

"Do you believe in destiny?"

What an odd question. She was immediately intrigued.

"Yes. Most of the time."

He smiled. "Then what are the odds that I would end up giving lectures at the same university you teach at?"

She thought about that.

"And did you intend to spend Christmas Eve at Swan's?"

"No." she remembered, and could feel the softest of smiles playing on her lips. "No, it was . . . the blizzard."

"Fate."

She didn't say anything.

"Destiny," Max said softly.

"Why were you there?" Realizing she was starving, she reached for her plate and tentatively tried a bite of turkey. Excellent, as was the stuffing.

"A friend recommended it highly. Kevin and I needed a few days' rest before coming to Middleton."

"Kevin?"

"My cat. He's a bigger curmudgeon than Crummond."

"How did you find out about that nickname?"

He grinned. "I'm a scientist. It's my job to observe things. To listen."

She thought about that. "Then this is...I'm...some kind of experiment?"

His expression sobered instantly. "No. No, I don't want you to think that."

"Then what is it?"

He leaned forward, taking her plate out of her nerveless fingers. She'd been just about to drop it.

"It's very simple, Eve. You take my breath away."

Stunned into silence, Eve could only stare at him.

"Now, if all you really wanted was that one night, the last thing in the world I'd want to do is make things miserable for you here at Middleton. So just say the word, and I'll back off."

She stared, unsure.

"But," he continued, "if you'd like to take this relationship along a different route and see what develops, that's what I'd like to do."

"But we . . . but we've . . ." Frustration assailed her. "You know, I'm not really sophisticated about things like this. What I did at Swan's—"

"I know. Me, too."

"You really don't always—" She paused.

"Nope."

Silence.

He smiled. "I told you. You take my breath away. I was putty in your hands."

She laughed then, and he looked relieved. He handed her back her plate, then picked up his.

"The meatballs are great," she said.

He tried one, then nodded his head.

"How can we go back to before—that?"

"Before the phenomenal sex?"

"Yes. Before—all that."

"We can't. We both know it's there. But I can promise you I'll behave like a gentleman. I won't pressure you. I'll let you take your time. I'll put that decision squarely in your hands, to do with what you will."

"Really?"

"Really."

"Are you a patient man?"

"When I want something badly enough."

That voice. Her plate started to slide again, and he caught it. "I'm not going to lie to you, Eve. I don't want to be just friends. I want you. Badly. You have no idea."

She couldn't breathe.

"I wanted you the night we met, and I didn't think you'd ask me to stay with you." He grinned. "And afterward, to be honest, I had a feeling you were going to bolt."

She could sense herself starting to bristle and he held up a placating hand.

"I knew I'd try to find you. I knew that what we'd shared—it wasn't ordinary, Eve. You have to admit that."

"No, I don't. I think that with your sex drive you could duplicate that night with any female on the planet."

He laughed.

"Seriously, Max, you'd have your choice. Did you see some of the looks you were getting from female faculty members downstairs?"

"What if I told you that you were wrong?"

"Ha! I don't think so."

"What if I told you that you bring out the best in me?" Now the grin he was giving her was positively lethal.

She blushed, then set her plate on the small table beside the couch. "*Sexually.* I bring out the best in you sexually. That's not enough to base a relationship on."

"It's a start."

"Men."

"No. Think about it. If the sex is great, most men will stick around long enough to build some kind of relationship. And the sex we had wasn't just great, I'd classify it as a five-star experience."

Now she could feel herself blushing even more, to the roots of her hair, her cheeks stinging with heat. Even though there was no one else in the vast library, she found herself whispering. "Do you have to be so graphic?"

"I'm telling you the truth. And I haven't even begun to get graphic. If you want a blow by blow—"

"Please, no!"

He laughed then, gently.

The conversation was interrupted by the appearance of Dr. Crummond at the door.

"How are you feeling, Eve?"

"Fine." She swung her legs over the side of the couch and sat up, tugging futilely at her short skirt. "I think I'm going to head on home early, if you don't mind."

"Oh, that's a shame. Glen and Patty are having such a good time—"

"I'll take her home," Max interjected smoothly.

Dead silence.

"All right," Dr. Crummond said, glancing from Eve back to Max. He seemed pleased that they were getting along so well.

"Max, I don't want you to miss out on a party planned in your honor. I can certainly call a cab—"

"No, it's fine. I'm a little tired from the move. I could use an early night. And besides, I'm sure I'll be spending many more evenings at your home, Dr. Crummond."

The department head beamed. "Of course, that would be splendid. Now, you two young people go on home. And drive carefully. The roads are still icy."

HIS CAR WAS a black Porsche.

He drove like a dream.

She felt both safe and unsafe with him.

And before she knew it, they were at her house.

"This is very nice," Max said as he opened the passenger side door and she stepped out onto the driveway. Eve had chosen not to wear boots, and now, with a light frosting of snow on her driveway, she felt decidedly unsteady in her high heels.

"Thank you." She took a few steps ahead of him and slipped.

He caught her beneath her arms. As she struggled to stand, she could feel her short skirt riding up. What had possessed her to wear a short jacket? She'd thrown it on before jumping straight into Glen's four-by-four, and had known he would drop her and Patty off right at Dr. Crummond's front door.

Now, as she slipped and slid, twisted and turned in the driveway, she managed to mash herself up against Max. She regained her balance, but immediately became supremely conscious of how their bodies pressed together as they stood alone outside her dark house.

Flakes of snow floated gently down. She looked up into his eyes, their lips a mere heartbeat apart.

He set her gently away from him.

She smiled brightly up at him, then turned and walked carefully up the drive toward her front door. She unlocked it, then turned in the doorway.

"Thank you for a wonderful—"

"I have something for you." He dug into the pocket of his black leather jacket and tossed an object toward her. As her hand came up automatically to catch it, she suspected. But the minute her fingers closed around the cellophane package, she knew.

Her goody bag.

He was grinning now. "It seemed a waste to leave all that chocolate at Swan's."

She didn't say anything, simply smiled. He looked adorable, standing out on her front porch. Snow fell in the background and she saw him try to suppress a shiver.

"I'm in charge, right?"

He held up his hand, fingers arranged in a Boy Scout's salute. "Scout's honor."

She sighed. "Come in."

SHE COULD SEE the scientist in him cataloging everything about her. The modern house, the way it was furnished, the fact that she hadn't put any covering on the large back windows that looked out over the birch trees. The framed posters on the walls, the fireplace and even Caliban as he pranced into the room and made a beeline for this fascinating stranger.

"Beautiful cat," he said, then reached down to scratch him behind his ears. The cat purred. Eve introduced them.

"Well," she said, taking off her jacket and examining the extent of the damage the wassail had done to her evening dress, "would you like some coffee?"

"That would be terrific."

"Give me just a minute. I'm going to change into something a little more—clean." She made a fast exit.

In her bedroom, she kicked off her heels and wondered what had possessed her to invite Max into her home.

Stop being such a fussbudget, she said to herself as she struggled with the zipper at the back of her dress. No way was she going to ask Max to come in and help her—and where had that thought come from?

Just stop it, she answered herself. *Stop those thoughts. I'm in control here. He's given me complete control. Nothing has to happen that I don't want to happen.* She'd peeled off the sexy dress, and now made short work of removing her stockings and bra.

Just wear something completely nonsexual. Try to look like someone's little sister. Like Gidget, or something. Buoyed by this thought, she rummaged through her dresser drawers until she came up with a set of forest green sweats. Pulling them on, she added thick gray slipper-socks, then brushed her hair back into a high ponytail.

Perfect. You look about twelve. Confident that she had everything under control, Eve headed toward the living room.

HE STUDIED THE BOOKS on her living room shelves while she was gone, holding Caliban in his arms the entire time. The lithe black cat purred and purred, pressing his head against Max's hand to demand more attention. Max scratched and studied.

They liked a lot of the same authors. That would make for interesting conversation.

Max knew the exact instant when she entered the room. He turned, and his first thought was that she looked absolutely adorable.

"Coffee," she muttered.

"Right." He fought to hide a grin. Eve was obviously nervous about having him inside her home, and he was determined to behave perfectly. The last thing he wanted to do was scare her off.

He followed her to the kitchen, liking what he saw. The kitchen was just as sleekly modern as the rest of her home, and he watched as she efficiently started the coffee. She set two mugs on the counter with sharp little bangs.

"Eve." He had to say something. "This isn't supposed to be some kind of endurance test."

She stopped, facing the kitchen counter, her back to him. He watched the rise and fall of her shoulders as she sighed.

"It's that obvious?"

"To me it is."

She turned toward him, bracing her hands behind her on the stark white counter. "Okay. You're right. I'll calm down."

"I want you to do whatever it is you want to do."

He thought he saw a slight gleam come into her eyes, but he wasn't sure.

"Why don't I sit over here while you finish preparing the coffee?"

"That would be fine."

SHE FELT like an absolute moron. Thirty-three and she couldn't have a man in for coffee without feeling as if she was about to come apart at the seams.

Not a man, a little voice inside her said. *This man.*

Because this man *really does something to you.* Eve had to consciously work to keep doubts and fears from surfacing.

Coffee. Just coffee. That's all. You can handle a cup of coffee and some cookies. Just pretend he's your neighbor or something. The boy next door...

She snuck a look at Max. *Never in a million years.* The analogy had been a bad one. Max wasn't one of the safe men she consciously surrounded herself with, and had even dated. There was something about him . . . She didn't even want to start analyzing it.

Eve carefully poured coffee into the two large mugs, then set out cream and sugar on a tray. She added a plate full of chocolate biscotti she'd bought at Patty's coffeehouse, The Brew-Ha-Ha, then carried the whole thing over to the small table in the corner of her large kitchen.

"It's a great view," Max commented. "Those birches."

"I love them. It's one of the reasons I rented this particular house."

He took his coffee black. She loaded hers with cream and sugar. He simply ate his biscotti, while she dunked hers to mush.

Too different, she thought.

Oh, please! that little voice answered. A wild little voice, and one she hadn't been paying too much attention to—except on Christmas Eve.

"Where are you going to be staying?" she asked, trying to get the conversational ball rolling. *Ask him to stay here*, that insidious little voice said. She smashed it down.

"I'm at the Middleton Inn at the moment. My stuff should be arriving any day, and Dr. Crummond has offered to take me around to see several houses that are for rent to faculty."

She nodded her head, pretending absolute fascination with her coffee and biscotti.

"Are there any houses around here?"

She gave him a look. His expression remained bland.

"I'd love a view like yours, Eve."

"There's one down the street, at two eighty-sex Oak Lane."

"Two eighty-six?"

"That's what I said."

"You said two eighty-sex."

"I did not."

"You did."

Eve stopped. Stared at him. Accepted defeat. She couldn't look at this man without thinking about the night they'd spent in bed together. That wonderful Christmas Eve. She'd replayed it in her mind a thousand, no, a million times. And probably blown it completely out of proportion.

"It couldn't have been as good as I remember," she said softly, her voice breathy. Catching.

"It was better. The real thing always is." His voice was so smoky. Sexy. And he was looking at her in a way that left no doubt he'd thought about that night as often as she had.

"I'd better be going," he said, and pushed away from the table, headed toward the door.

Ask him to stay. . . .

"What if I asked you to stay?"

Silence. But he stopped. Turned.

"What?"

It wasn't until he answered her that she realized she'd asked the question out loud. She took her courage in both hands and asked again.

"What if I told you I wanted you to stay?"

"Eve—" Now he looked decidedly uneasy.

"You said that particular decision was in my hands, didn't you?"

He ran his fingers through his dark hair. "I don't want you to do something you're going to regret in the morning."

"Okay. Fair enough." She rose from her chair and walked to the center of the kitchen. He was only a few feet away, in the doorway leading to the hall. "What if I told you that I wanted to have sex with you one more time so I could convince myself that it simply couldn't have been that great? What if I asked you to prove to me it was as good as I thought it was?"

"*What!*" Now she had his attention.

"You heard what I said."

"Let me get this straight," he said, and she knew she'd managed to light his fuse. "You can't believe that what happened that night at Swan's was all that terrific—am I getting it right?"

"Yes . . . that's about . . . that's right."

"So you want an instant replay, tonight, on the spot, in order to make up your mind if you want to continue participating in this relationship. Right?"

"Right."

"Eve, you play hardball."

She swallowed.

He smiled, slowly, looking at her as if he wanted to eat her up. "Talk about performance anxiety—"

It was the craziest thing, as if that wild little voice inside her were goading her into action.

"Well, if you don't think you're up to it—"

The silence between them was deadly.

She watched as the fingers of his right hand bit into the wooden frame of the door.

"Eve, what are you playing at?"

"This is no game."

"Tell me what you really want."

She swallowed against the excitement building in her throat. "I want you, for tonight, to take the choice out of my hands." She hesitated. "I want you to want me."

"I do."

"Then—" The words hung unspoken in the still air.

"Last chance," he said, that deep, rough voice so calm and quiet.

She couldn't speak.

"Tell me what you want, Eve."

"You."

HE KNEW THAT if he slept with her tonight, he'd lose her. Not that he didn't want to sleep with Eve. Every cell in his body hummed, every muscle tensed, every primitive masculine impulse told him to pick her up and carry her to her bedroom.

And ravish her. Make her his.

But Max was a scientist, and one of his gifts was the ability to coolly and calmly size up a situation. As much as he wanted Eve, he had to make sure he didn't scare her off. And the way he wanted her would scare her off.

I want you…to take the choice out of my hands….

Truly primal, feminine words. He thought he understood where the impulse was coming from. But if he pushed her too far tonight, he'd never see her again. Guaranteed.

On Christmas Eve, she'd responded to him the way she had because she'd known it was a one-night stand. She'd thought she would never see him again, never have to face him. That guaranteed anonymity had freed her in a way that would have been impossible if they'd met any other time.

In the confines of her room at the inn, they'd communicated with each other in the most basic way possible. Had reached way beyond what was normal for the short time they'd known each other. Now his instincts were telling him if he wanted her to give herself to him in the same way for the long term, he had to start over. Go slow. Be gentle.

Tame the beast. In both of them.

"Eve," he said, stepping away from the door frame. He closed the short distance between them, until he was standing in front of her, looking down at her upturned face. "Eve, I don't think we should do this." He paused.

She waited.

Masculine pride forced the next sentence out. "And it's not because I don't think I'm . . . up to it."

She sighed, unable to meet his eyes. "That was truly a low blow, and I regret saying it."

He smiled. "Okay. Here's what I think. I think we should start over. Slow things way down. Get to know each other."

She looked up at him, and he almost laughed out loud at the suspicious look in those beautiful green eyes, swiftly followed by relief. She was so open, his Eve. So easy to read. "Those are supposed to be my lines."

He pulled her into his arms, then tucked her head beneath his chin. "Like, I feel so cheap, sordid, degraded—"

She started to laugh as she placed her hand over his mouth, stilling his words. He could feel her relax and knew everything would be all right. For now.

But the feel of her palm against his lips, her scent, her skin . . . Without conscious volition, he placed his hand over hers, pressing it against his lips, and kissed her palm. He watched her face as she turned it up toward him, saw the dreamy expression in her green eyes.

And knew they were both in for a hard lesson in self-control.

THE FEEL OF HIS LIPS on her palm brought to mind everything they'd already shared. And then some.

Oh, that body. Its potency had amazed her. And her own body's reaction had surprised her. She'd never felt this way with any other man. Eve wondered at how, in its infinite wisdom, her body had simply decided to wake up at the age of thirty-three and go into sensual overdrive. Maybe she'd starved her senses far too long.

All she knew was that she wanted to rip her clothes off, and his, and do what her human sexuality students laughingly referred to as "the horizontal watusi" right here on the kitchen floor.

She just didn't care. And there was a part of her that gloried in the swift, hot response this man could so effortlessly call forth from the deepest part of her.

He pulled her closer and she went willingly, stepping inside his parted, jean-clad legs and running a trembling hand over his jawline. He hesitated just a fraction of a second before his lips came down over hers.

What a kiss. Lights behind her closed eyes. Knees shaking. Warmth pooling in her most sexual spots. Yearning. Desire slipped into her bloodstream, leaving her body soft and pliable. Willing. Such excitement, such raw, pure feeling. Chemistry. Whatever you called it, it was there.

She'd been afraid to serve him coffee, but she wasn't at all afraid to see him naked, let him take all her clothes off, be as intimate as possible with him. None of it made sense, but as her brain shorted out whenever he touched her, none of it had to make sense—right now.

He eased her lips apart, slipped his tongue inside her mouth, and moved it in such a blatantly sexual way, she whimpered against his lips. Wanting more. Not caring. She felt like the woman in the commercial, who wears a bun and thick glasses, then tears off those glasses and whips down her hair.

She just wanted to be with him. The urge was so strong. So primitive. It didn't make sense, and she, a professor who taught her students to make intelligent choices about their sexuality, finally understood what women had been up against since the beginning of time.

She sensed his control almost break before he set her away from him, holding her waist, his grip feeling tense. Both of them took deep breaths, then she pushed down her shyness and looked him straight in the eye.

He smiled down at her, but she could see it was with effort.

"Couldn't have been that good, huh?" he whispered.

She started to grin.

"Eve, you have no idea what you do to me."

She couldn't lie to this man, not when he was being this emotionally open with her.

"Me, too. To me, I mean."

"I know."

"But," she said, carefully placing a palm on his chest, feeling the muscles tighten beneath his black sweater, "I like what you said about going slow. Starting over. It makes me feel—safe."

"I know." He took her hand, kissed it, stepped away. "I'll call you tomorrow."

"All right." She just stood there, looking up at him, then realized she should see him to the door. Max simply reduced her brains to mush.

"I can see myself out," he said as he backed out of the kitchen, keeping his eyes on her. "Oh, thanks for the coffee."

"You're welcome."

He nodded his head. Smiled.

She smiled back. "Get going before I do something I may regret."

"Yes, ma'am." He paused. "Happy New Year, Eve."

"You, too."

He turned and headed for her front door.

OUTSIDE, in the cold crisp air, snowflakes all around, Max climbed into his Porsche, started the engine and let it warm up. As he gazed out the windshield at Eve's house, the testosterone-driven part of his brain wondered if he'd been crazy to follow the course of action he'd chosen. Yes, it was nobler, and kinder—but damned uncomfortable. Not to mention frustrating.

He smiled as he backed the car out of her driveway. Winning Eve over, body and soul, wouldn't be easy. But it would be worth it.

INSIDE, in the warmth of her bedroom, Eve stared at the clock. Eleven-thirty. Gail would still be up. She could call with the pretext of wishing her friend a Happy New Year, or she could get down to what was really bothering her. Without stopping to let doubt creep in, she dialed her friend's phone number. Gail was one of those "you-can-call-me-at-four-in-the-morning" kind of friends.

"Gail? Me." Eve took a deep breath. "I have to ask your opinion about something." She took another breath, trying to still the unsettled feeling in her stomach. Feeling this vulnerable was a new sensation for her. But Gail would understand.

"Well, it has to do with a one-night stand...."

4

MAX WOKE UP in his room at the Middleton Inn on New Year's Day, slipped silently into the bathroom and took a quick shower. He did everything in his power not to wake an exhausted Kevin. The tabby cat lay beneath the down comforter, looking totally wiped out. Tooting horns and fireworks at midnight had taken their toll. The cat's silvery gray-and-black fluffy tail barely showed from underneath the thick spread.

He thought of Eve as he dried off. One other thing that the scientist in him had observed had fascinated him. While her house was as starkly modern as they came, her bedroom—which he'd peeked into on the way out—was utterly feminine. A sanctuary. And a major clue to the real Eve, the woman she didn't allow many people to see.

The woman she'd let him see on Christmas Eve.

As Max pulled on his jeans and sweater, he thought of her and smiled. What a woman. Charming. Tempestuous. Unpredictable. Sexy as hell. And she'd probably have a complete change of mind concerning their relationship by the time she got up this morning.

That was all right by him. He was nothing if not persistent. And he was rather proud that their kiss had been—well, proof that Christmas Eve hadn't been some sort of fluke. He hoped she'd remember it.

Once in the suite's living room, Max found his black leather jacket and headed out the door.

EVE YAWNED and rolled over on her back, then stretched.

What a night.

Alexander Maximillian Elliott was no slouch as a kisser. She had to wonder at herself, getting all worked up like that. Getting *him* all worked up. Challenging him with a sexual dare of sorts. What had she been thinking?

Prove to me it was as good as I thought it was. How had Max been able to resist a challenge like that?

She yawned again, totally exhausted. How had Max found the strength to give her a kiss like that, then leave? But she already knew the answer even as she thought of the question. Because he'd been thinking of her. And what was right for her. And teasing her. Daring her to make up her mind for good about him.

So here she was the next morning, still turned on, excited, looking forward to seeing him again and talking to him on the phone—and still scared.

"Of course you're scared," Gail had said comfortingly last night. "I was terrified when Jerry came into my life, because some little voice in my head told me he was the one. Before that, I'd dated a bunch of losers because I hadn't wanted to get close to anyone. But when you know, you know."

Eve wondered if she knew. In her heart, yes. But her head, ah, her head. That was where all the trouble started.

The mattress depressed slightly as Caliban jumped up on the bed. He trotted up by her head, circled the pillow, then plopped down next to her, purring loudly.

She scratched him beneath his chin, then yawned again. There was nothing she had to do today; she might as well sleep in. Eve closed her eyes and smiled.

You'd better sleep. You have no idea what Mad Max is going to think up next.

MAX WALKED INTO TOWN. Middleton University had been built around one wide path that bisected the entire campus, which was small to begin with. The university was proud of its professor-student ratio, the way each student was given lots of personal attention. And it was a lovely campus, with giant old trees and gently rolling hills surrounding the brick and stone buildings.

Now he walked up that middle path, his boots crunching through the hard-packed snow. He was on his way to the post office, which was one of the main social gathering spots. Everyone on campus had a

P.O. box, there was no general delivery except to the post office, located right across the street from the dean's offices and the college bookstore.

He let himself inside, then opened his mailbox. He hadn't checked it in a couple of days, and smiled when he recognized Annie's familiar scrawl on a blue envelope. She was living in France with her husband, a history professor, and their three children. With any luck, he might get over there this spring and see them all.

A few fliers and a note from Dr. Crummond. He threw away the junk mail, stuffed the correspondence into one of his pockets, then headed out the door into the bright winter sunshine. Max stood in front of the post office, on the snow-covered sidewalk, and wondered what to do next.

He could call Dr. Crummond and look at a few houses.

He could go back to the Middleton Inn and see what was on their lunch menu.

What he really wanted to do was return to Eve's house, climb into that feminine, frilly bed with her and wake her up in the nicest way possible. He'd never been able to understand most men's fascination with sports on New Year's Day when there were so many better ways to be entertained.

But he didn't really have that right. He also had a feeling Eve needed some time to assimilate what had happened last night. He wasn't such a dodo when it came to the fairer sex that he couldn't realize she had a lot of emotional baggage, and some considerable fears about relationships. So Max was headed toward the inn for an early lunch when a familiar voice called out.

"Max! Hey, Max!"

He glanced over and saw Patty in the doorway of one of the shops fronting Main Street, right between the campus bookstore and the Middleton Inn. The swinging sign above her head read The Brew-Ha-Ha. He started toward her, glad for the company. He needed some time away from his thoughts.

"What are you doing here?" he asked. "It's New Year's Day."

She laughed. "I'm not open for business. I just have some shipments to unload if I want to be ready for the week ahead. Students will be coming back as early as the fifth, even though classes don't start until the tenth."

"What do you have to do?"

"I've got tons of coffee and tea that has to be unpacked, shelves that have to be restocked, some pottery that has to be put in the front window and just general cleaning. Want a cup of coffee? I was going to have one before I started."

He reached the door of the coffeehouse when he answered. "Sure. Where's Glen?"

"Home watching the Rose Bowl." She made a face. "I'm not into sports."

"Me, either. Coffee sounds great."

Max realized from reading the sign inside the door that the coffee bar was also a comedy club. It seemed deserted in the bright winter sunlight. This was the sort of place one always imagined after dark, with the scent of ground coffee beans filling the air and the rollicking laughter of students making the club come alive. Their attention would be focused on the stand-up comedian on the small stage down front.

The inside walls were of gently faded red brick, with large philodendron and spider plants hanging from the ceiling. Framed movie posters graced the walls, along with shelves filled with coffee and tea paraphernalia. There were even books along some of the shelves, and a rack full of newspapers.

Max noticed three computers along one wall.

"What are those for?"

"The Web. And the Internet. We're a full-service shop. People can leave E-mail—that sort of thing."

"What a great idea," Max said as Patty poured him an oversize mug of coffee.

"French roast. That okay with you?"

"Perfect."

She put a plate of almond croissants and some cream and sugar on the table between them, then sat down.

"The Brew-Ha-Ha used to be one of those intellectual-type coffee shops. The place intimidated people terribly. You had to be a poet or literary writer to fit in. Terribly pretentious. So when the owner died and his son put it up for sale, my dad loaned Glen and I the money to buy it. I envisioned it as a place where people could come for a great cup of coffee and a few laughs."

"You had a terrific vision."

"Thanks." She chewed thoughtfully on a croissant, and he could see the wheels turning. One of the great benefits, Max thought, about having a female fraternal twin, was that he knew a little bit more about the female mind than most men.

"What's on your mind?" Patty asked.

He decided not to hedge the obvious.

"Eve."

"I knew it! The attraction between the two of you was . . . explosive. Intense. Straight out of a romance novel."

"We've met before."

"Really? Like in a past life?"

"No. This one."

"That sly dog! She didn't tell me."

"I think she was a little shocked to see me again."

"She wasn't happy?"

"No." He paused. "I want to get to know her better, but she's . . . prickly. She may not appreciate me talking to you like this. But I need to figure out what's standing in my way."

Her eyes were admiring. "You get right to the point."

"It gets results."

She fluttered her hands, picked up a second croissant. "All the way home, I kept telling Glen that the
two of you would be perfect for each other!"

"I just wish Eve would think so. Do you mind my
pumping you for information?"

"Not at all. All's fair, as they say." She narrowed her
eyes, studied him. "Though I have to admit, I
wouldn't come clean for any old guy. You're special."

"Thanks."

"No, I mean it. And as for Eve, well, she's one of
my dearest friends. If I thought you were up to no
good, I wouldn't tell you a thing." She leaned closer.
"But it's my personal opinion that she's been alone too
long. She's a real people person, a deep feeler, and it's
not good for her."

"I agree. Tell me about her mother." Max took a sip
of the hot coffee. It was excellent. "And any serious
relationships she's had that you know about."

"Oh, Dr. Elliott, you're in for an earful."

AFTER HIS TALK with Patty, Max returned to his room
at the Middleton Inn. He'd been given one of the larger
rooms that overlooked Main Street below, and now
he stood by the window and studied the serene, snow-
covered campus. The bare tree branches looked
starkly beautiful against the leaden January sky.

Kevin grumbled from beneath the bed. He'd been
upset at receiving his breakfast so late this morning,

even though he had a good supply of his favorite dry food in a bowl in the bathroom. This was one cat that didn't like having his routine changed.

"I wonder how you'll get along with Caliban," Max had said to him as he dished out the wet food. Kevin had merely swished his bushy tail and gotten down to the serious business of eating. He was an enormous, fluffy, dark gray tabby cat. Max had found him on the side of the road, soaked, during a thunderstorm. He'd taken the cat in, and Kevin had proved to be good company, if a tad grumpy.

Now, as Max studied the scene outside his window, he wondered what he was going to do about Eve. *He* knew what he wanted. She was the wild card. He'd have to proceed with utmost caution, so as not to scare her away. She was such a contrast of emotions—warm and wild in bed, cool and reserved otherwise.

He understood a lot more about her since his talk with Patty. The father that had left her young mother pregnant, alone and afraid. Eve's parents had never married, but Mary Anne Vaughn had done an outstanding job of raising her only daughter. It didn't take a psychiatrist to understand why Eve devoted a good part of her life to studying human sexuality. And to teaching young women the importance of having knowledge about their own reproductive systems.

How strange, that he'd chosen the same path. When his twin had accidentally become pregnant, their entire family had been thrown into an uproar. His father had demanded to know who the young, prospective father was, but Annie had kept that secret to herself.

Max had known who the father was. At sixteen, he hadn't possessed any scruples where his emotions were concerned. He'd found Tommy Chadwick and given him the fight of his life. He'd pounded him good, for using and abusing his sister. And never, ever mentioned the incident to Annie. It still wasn't something he was terribly proud of, but he'd been hurting for his twin and it had seemed like the only way to release his pain. And avenge Annie.

When her baby had been stillborn, he'd responded to her pain, to his family's pain, with a silent mission in life. The Cyber Baby had been born.

Fate. Destiny. He and Eve had been on the same path for a long time.

Patty had told him more. How close Eve and her mother had been. How they'd genuinely liked each other. Mary Anne had only been seventeen when Eve was born, so she'd been a young mother. But she'd been extraordinarily compassionate and strong. Yet Eve had told Patty that she'd known her mother had given up a lot for her. It was something she didn't want to see repeated in any other young woman's life.

How different his own life had been. Every day, his mother and father had shown him how wonderful a good marriage could be. How life affirming and enriching. How much fun. It was something he'd always wanted for himself, somewhere along the line. As soon as he fell in love.

He'd always been thankful for Annie, too, and his relationship with her. Having a twin sister had made him extraordinarily aware of what women went through. And he found, as he hit puberty, he was not only fascinated with women but sincerely liked them.

He'd gone through a whole slew of girlfriends in high school and college, then graduate work had slowed down his amorous pursuits for a while. But not for long. Before Eve, he'd played the field. Yet he'd always been honest with his women, loved them all. One at a time, of course. He had a strong sense of honor in relationships, but he hadn't been able to commit until he could feel he was sincerely in love.

Then Christmas Eve, meeting Eve, that magical night . . . He'd fallen for her long before she'd let him take her to bed, but their night of passion had solidified it. Now, he felt it was only a matter of time—and winning her trust. This relationship would make it, depending on whether or not Eve could have faith in both him and herself.

Max walked away from the window and sat down in one of the soft, overstuffed chairs in the bedroom suite. He put his feet up on a plump hassock, then smiled as Kevin leapt up onto his knee. The enormous tabby circled once, twice, then settled into his lap. Max rubbed the top of his head as he thought.

Eve hadn't really had the sort of life that led a woman to have a whole lot of faith in men.

There were two relationships that Patty had been aware of. Both were almost templates of the casual, noncommitted style of the nineties. Neither had lasted. Neither of those men, Patty had told him, was the strong, solid type. "Like you or Glen," she'd said.

Then, her eyes sparkling, she'd told him, "I guess since I know one of your secrets, you should know one of mine."

He'd sensed she was heartbreakingly eager to confide in someone, and he gave her all his attention.

"I'm pregnant."

"Congratulations!"

"But you can't tell anyone." Briefly, she'd told him that even her husband didn't know. After three miscarriages, Glen hadn't wanted to try again.

"He saw how much it took out of me," Patty had confided, stirring her decaf. "But I decided to throw caution to the wind, you know? Sometimes you just have to take a leap of faith."

"I know that feeling. When are you going to tell him?"

She'd smiled. "By next week I'm past my first trimester, the scariest part. My doctor says I can tell Glen then, because he thinks I'm going to be lucky this time."

He'd studied her, admiring her extraordinary courage. Patty's situation gave new meaning to the expression "Where there's life, there's hope."

"I have a good feeling about this," he'd told her. "And your secret's safe with me."

Max felt confident that Patty's assessment of his character was correct. He was the sort who, once he'd fallen in love, was in for the long haul. Who wouldn't up and leave at the first sign of trouble. He knew he could be counted on, just as he knew Eve was the sort of woman who would display incredible loyalty and devotion.

Now, the only problem he had was convincing her of that.

HE CALLED HER late that afternoon.

"Eve? I was wondering if you'd like to join me for dinner at the Middleton Inn."

He could hear the hesitation over the phone line.

"I . . . I don't know. . . ."

Fear had many shades to it. He was a patient man. He'd discover what her fear was and help her get over it.

"Just dinner."

He heard her sigh.

"Max. I feel so ashamed."

"About what?" Now he was intrigued. And concerned.

"What I did last night. Goading you into kissing me. It was . . . childish and immature."

"And a terrific challenge. Keeps me on my toes." He took a deep breath. "I think you should take me up on dinner. I hear the Canadian cheese soup is out of this world."

She hesitated.

"We could stop by The Brew-Ha-Ha afterward and have a cup of coffee by that big fireplace."

"It's closed."

"Patty's working late. I know she'd open it up for us."

He felt her hesitation again.

"On my honor, I'll keep us in public places so we won't have a repeat of last night's kiss. Or anything else."

Silence.

He took another deep breath. "Not that I wouldn't like a repeat. Anytime, anyplace. But I meant what I said—you're setting the pace."

"You know, you could find yourself a woman on this campus who was a lot less neurotic."

"But then she wouldn't be you."

Silence again. Fear. He counted to five. "Do you like cheese soup?"

"I love it, and it is fantastic."

"Then come have dinner with me."

A short struggle, then to his delight she said, "What time?"

"Six?"

"Fine."

"I'll pick you up."

"I'll meet you there."

He knew when to compromise. "But I'll see you back home."

"All right."

EVE SPENT an extraordinarily long amount of time deciding what to wear. The inn was a casual sort of place, with a college campus sort of style. Nice jeans and a comfy sweater wouldn't have been out of place, but she decided on a long gray skirt, boots and a chunky hand-knit sweater in shades of gray, blue and lilac. She pulled her hair back into a conservative little twist, and the only jewelry she chose to wear was a pair of pearl studs.

The trouble was, she liked Max. A lot. But it wasn't that simple for her. Relationships were the one area of her life she hadn't quite mastered. But he'd promised her they would go slow, that he'd let her set the pace, and she was grateful for that.

She arrived at the inn promptly at six, to be shown to a table in the far corner. Max was already there, and he rose from his seat when he saw her. She sat, he sat, then he handed her a menu.

"They say the turkey's good," he said.

"I'm kind of turkied out after the holidays."

"I know what you mean."

A short silence.

"The fish sounds good," she said.

"The salmon?"

"Yes."

Safe, safe, so safe. She couldn't believe that this was the same man she'd spent Christmas Eve in bed with. She knew so very much about him physically. Yet there was a lot more, emotionally, she still needed to know.

She ordered the salmon. He ordered a steak. They both ordered the cheese soup, and salads. Max ordered the wine. Once their waiter left, with the menus, she found herself alone at the table with Max.

"I don't bite," he said, his tone mild.

"I know. You're actually quite a nice man."

"Uh-oh, the kiss of death."

"I mean that in the best possible way."

"I'd rather be the rogue, alpha male."

She smiled. Sociobiology she understood. "You are a rogue." She liked the way his eyes lit up at that. "A dangerous sort of guy."

He leaned back in his chair. "Dangerous enough."

Their salads arrived, so for a short time they were preoccupied. Then their soup. During their soup a heavy rain began to fall, sheeting the windows and making the streets slick and dangerous.

"I don't like weather like this," Eve said, looking outside at the trees lining Middle Path. "I can't help thinking about all the students coming back to campus after Christmas vacation."

"Maybe it will let up."

"It looks pretty nasty."

She enjoyed dinner. Max kept both the conversation and the excellent wine flowing. He asked her questions about her classes, what she had planned for the semester, what texts she used, what the focus of her graduate seminar was going to be.

Eve found she liked talking to him. He was intelligent and insightful, and made her laugh. That, combined with a body that didn't quit, an insatiable sexual curiosity and phenomenal stamina, made her aware that this was a man she could fall deeply in love with.

At which thought she froze.

"Something in the fish?" he asked, and she realized he'd misinterpreted the expression on her face.

"No, it's excellent," she replied, forcing herself to relax. For a distraction, she looked out the window. The rain was still pounding down outside, and Eve knew what that water would do to the streets once it froze over. Driving would be treacherous.

In direct contrast, this was such an incredibly nice evening. The exquisite food, candlelight, the nearby fireplace offering its warmth. Outside, the world was cold, dark and icy, while in this dining room she could simply try to relax and enjoy Max.

Eve decided, at that moment, that she would make a real effort to get to know this man. She believed him when he said they would take things slow. She genuinely liked him. For once, she wouldn't anticipate a disaster, she'd simply see where the relationship led.

They were shown various desserts, and Eve hesitated.

"Did you still want to go over to The Brew-Ha-Ha?"

Max shook his head. "I don't really want to go outside at all in weather like this."

He had a point. The rain showed no sign of letting up. It was promising to be a nasty night.

"Then I'll have the apple pie," she said. "À la mode."

"The chocolate ice-cream brownie pie for me."

That decision made, they simply watched the rain come down. Coffee followed dessert, and Eve knew it was time to thank Max for a wonderful evening. Then the lights went out. This was followed by a rumble of thunder, then a vivid streak of lightning.

Several patrons at nearby tables gasped their approval of the celestial show. Eve hated storms, and gripped the seat of her chair with both hands.

"Eve?" Max's tone was very gentle.

She closed her eyes. "I don't like this."

He moved to sit in the chair next to her, then enfolded one of her hands in his. His felt very warm, so she knew hers was icy cold.

"Annie doesn't like storms, either," he remarked. "They scared her to death when we were kids."

"I suppose you enjoy them."

"I love them."

"I knew it."

Thunder boomed again, and she felt as if she were cowering. "I hate being this way, but—"

"Don't apologize. You don't have to. Not with me."

She didn't say anything, simply waited for the answering crack of lightning. Max signed the dinner bill to his room, then Eve watched as he reached into the pocket of his jacket and took out a slim, black metallic flashlight.

"Were you a Boy Scout?"

He grinned. "Always prepared."

They started toward the door, but when Eve saw how hard the rain was falling, she hesitated. Max must have sensed it, because he paused.

"We can wait until the storm lets up," he suggested. "There's a great fireplace in the parlor."

"I don't want to keep you up all evening."

"Not a problem."

They sat in the parlor, by the light and warmth of the fire. The innkeeper and his wife were lighting candles throughout the house, and Eve thought how unbearably romantic all this was. It seemed perfect that Max was the man by her side.

Twenty minutes later, the rain showed no signs of letting up.

"I can wait down here, you know," she began. "Isn't all your stuff arriving tomorrow? That means it'll be a busy day for you."

"Don't worry about it." He was sitting back on the couch, relaxed, while she felt as if every nerve in her body was tightly wired. At least the thunder and lightning had stopped. Now all they could hear was the sound of rain drumming on the roof.

"I have a suggestion," Max began.

She turned toward him.

"What do you have to do tomorrow?"

She thought for a moment. "I planned on going by the bookstore to check and see if all the texts I ordered came in. Then I was going to go over some of my lesson plans. Just basically start getting ready for the tenth."

"Why don't you stay with me tonight?"

The images that simple question conjured up were highly erotic.

"Oh, Max, I don't think so."

"No sex. Just sleep."

"I . . . well . . . I could always get another room."

"They're full up."

She knew he was telling her the truth. The Middleton Inn was not an enormous establishment. It had only eight guest rooms, and they were usually full over the Christmas vacation and early January. Often parents came back early with students, wanting a chance to share some time on campus with their children.

Eve bit her lip, stared at the fire. It seemed an unnecessary hardship to drag Max out into the rain during a storm like this. During the winter in Ohio, the weather was highly unpredictable. Not only would he have to see her home, he'd have to come back to his room at the inn.

Her decision was made for her when the innkeeper came into the parlor. "Just wanted you folks to know, there's a tree down around Oak Lane. The fire department's been called, but I don't think they'll have it cleared away until morning."

"Thank you," Max said.

Eve nodded her head. "I'll stay with you."

The smile he gave her was a wry one. "Why do you say that in the tone of voice of someone headed for the guillotine?"

She laughed then. Taking his hand in hers, she linked their fingers. His felt strong and warm. Solid. "It's okay," she said, looking up at him. "I want to stay."

MAX RECOGNIZED that this evening was a precious gift.

There was no better way to win Eve's trust than to spend an evening with her and not have it turn into something sexual. If they could make it through the night without getting intimate, it might convince her he truly intended to let her set the pace of their relationship.

Now, with only the slender flashlight for illumination, he unlocked the door to his room and ushered her inside. The lights still hadn't come up. In fact, the innkeeper had told them they would be lucky to regain power by morning.

"You take the bed. Kevin and I can take the floor."

"Oh, I couldn't do that to you."

"I insist."

She stood very still, just inside the door, as he entered farther into the large bedroom. Finding a book of matches, he lit a fat red candle on the side table by the large, queen-size bed. The scents of cinnamon and clove filled the air.

"It smells like the bed and breakfast," Eve remarked.

"It should. I bought this candle from their gift shop."

"Oh."

He wondered if she was remembering that first night. He certainly was.

"Well—" he turned to look at her "—would you like a shirt or something? To sleep in."

"That would be wonderful."

He found her one of his warm, flannel shirts, in a black watch pattern. She took it into the bathroom to change, and he used the opportunity to turn the covers down on the large, comfortable bed.

Kevin promptly jumped up and snuggled against the pillows.

"No! Tonight you'll be sleeping with me—"

"That's all right. I've never minded cats."

He turned, Kevin struggling to get out of his arms. And saw Eve, in his shirt. It came down to midthigh on her petite frame, she'd buttoned every single button and rolled up the sleeves. She'd also taken her vibrant hair down from its severe style.

In his opinion, she looked sexy as sin.

His rampant thoughts must not have shown on his face because she showed full trust in him, stepping right up to him and taking the struggling, stubborn Kevin out of his arms.

"You must be Kevin," she said, then started to pet the enormous, fluffy cat. Kevin purred, then snuggled against her full breasts, giving Max a contented look.

Max knew he had it bad when he was jealous of his own damn cat.

"The bed," he said, directing her to it with a sweep of his hand.

"Thank you." Eve, Kevin still in her arms, slid beneath the covers and settled herself in for the night.

"Does he like to sleep above or underneath the covers?"

"Who?" As rational as he was being about all this, Max found sexual frustration was impeding his brain's functions.

"Kevin."

"He'll let you know." This was going to be a lot harder than he'd thought. Eve, with just his shirt and possibly nothing else on, and in his bed, was driving him crazy. She looked incredible, her face scrubbed free of makeup, that gorgeous tumble of dark auburn hair framing that angelic little face. What had possessed him to come up with this plan? He should have seen her home tonight even if he'd had to rent a dog sled.

"Max?"

"Hmm?"

"Don't you want to get ready for bed?"

That simple little question fired his imagination and raced it into overdrive. "Yeah. Sure." He left the room, seeking the sanctuary of the bathroom. Once inside, he realized he had no idea what he was going to wear tonight, as he hadn't owned a single pair of pajamas since he'd been a teenager.

Great.

The next thought made him groan out loud and sit down on the side of the tub, his head in his hands.

Well, he did have a pair of pajamas. Only they weren't what he would have normally picked out for himself. The Elliotts were a great family for gag gifts. He and Annie were the family champions, and the gift she'd mailed to him early in December before his move had made him laugh out loud when he'd opened it.

She'd given him a pair of very sexy, red silk pajamas. The card had been signed, "Merry Christmas, Hef," a reference to Hugh Hefner, the founder of *Playboy* magazine, who was reputed to have spent most of his life in similar silk pj's. Annie had apparently chosen the gag gift in the hopes of helping Max get a little action into his life.

Little did she know.

Well, he had no choice. He couldn't prance out there in his underwear. He couldn't wear his sweats, either, that would surely be overcompensating.

He'd bite the bullet and wear the damn pajamas.

As quietly as he could, he opened the bathroom and headed into the candlelit bedroom.

"Max? Is something wrong?"

"Nothing. Nothing at all." He retrieved the silk pajamas from his suitcase and headed back into the bathroom. Stripping off his clothes, he put them on. The silk felt incredibly sensual against his bare skin, and made him remember the way Eve's naked body had felt against his.

The inevitable occurred, and Max gritted his teeth. Using all the control he could muster, he waited until his aroused state wasn't blatantly obvious, then sauntered out into the bedroom.

HE WAS STUNNING. Absolutely stunning. Her mouth went dry at the sight of him in red silk, strolling into the candlelit bedroom as if he owned the place. As if he were master of all he surveyed and didn't have a care in the world.

Eve bit her lip against the little moan, the slight squeak that escaped her. She closed her eyes and feigned sleep.

And itched.

She kept her eyes determinedly closed, as she heard Max opening the closet door. He had to be getting extra blankets and pillows down, to create some sort of makeshift bed on the floor.

She itched. And felt guilty.

She heard him finish making up his bed, then lie down on the floor.

"Eve?"

"Yes?"

"Would you blow out the candle?"

"Certainly. Kevin, I'm just going to move a little bit, okay?" The large tabby cat purred loudly, the sound filling the quiet room.

She heard a soft snort from the direction of the floor.

"What?"

"Nothing." But Max sounded strange, as if he were gritting his teeth.

She blew out the candle, plunging the room into darkness. Eve lay back and Kevin cuddled up against her once again. She tried to breathe deeply and forget that the handsomest man she'd ever met was lying less than five feet away from her.

She itched again. Scratched.

Was absolutely miserable.

"Max?"

"Eve?"

"I itch."

Dead silence.

"Don't do this to me, Eve."

She understood his meaning instantly, and knew he misunderstood her. "No, I mean this wool flannel itches. I have to take it off. I can wear some wools against my skin, but others—"

He was up out of his pile of blankets in a second, then swiftly unbuttoned the red silk pajama top and handed it to her. "This should be more comfortable."

"Okay." She took the top out of his hands, thankful the room was so dark, she could barely make out his naked chest. That would have been sheer sensual torture. Here she was, the woman who wanted to go slow, who didn't want to rush things, getting incredibly turned on by Max's invisible muscled chest.

He had an unfair advantage over her.

"Um . . . do you have that flashlight?"

"Here." He handed it to her.

She turned it on, then made a hasty exit to the bathroom. Inside, she doffed the flannel shirt, then made a quick decision and stepped inside the shower.

HE LISTENED to the sound of the water and fantasized. Eve, naked, the water sluicing over that voluptuous little body. Eve, in the red silk top, all wet from the spray, the drenched silk outlining her hard little nipples. Eve, reaching for him, beckoning him into the stall with her, taking the soap, sliding her hands all over his body...

By the time she entered the dark bedroom, he was more than ready for action. And regretting the day he'd ever told her all sexual decisions were in her hands.

SHE ENTERED the bedroom cautiously, not turning on the small flashlight. Eve didn't want to wake Max. He had to be asleep by now. She'd taken a long, warm shower, knowing it was the only way to stop the itching. She'd always had extremely sensitive skin and couldn't use most commercial detergents and soaps. Now, thoroughly rinsed, dried and clad only in the red silk pajama top, she knew she was in for a restful night.

If only she could stop thinking about Max.

That chest. That man. *That night*...

Thoughts of him had tormented her in the shower. When she finally entered the bedroom she was sexually aroused, thinking about Max and knowing she had absolutely no right to ask him to do anything with her.

For heaven's sake, she was a modern woman. Surely they could share a bedroom for a night and not obsess about sex? Surely both of them were that mature at least?

So Eve headed in the direction she thought the bed was, promptly caught her toe on one of the blankets on the floor, and fell full-length on top of Max.

5

HE'D BEEN THINKING wicked sexual thoughts when she landed on him, so hard against his chest that she almost knocked the breath out of him. Almost. His hands came up instinctively to steady her. Unfortunately, her shirt had ridden up when she fell, so what his hands fell upon were her naked buttocks.

Time stood perfectly still.

"Are you all right?" he whispered into the darkness. He knew he'd probably cushioned the worst of her fall, but he couldn't be sure. He found himself relishing this accidental contact, the feel of her full breasts against his chest, her belly pressed against his hard and painful arousal.

"Yes." She started to get up off him and stopped.

"Max," she said, and he loved the way his name sounded on her lips, all breathy and sensual.

"Yes?" He'd play by her rules, only he was hoping against hope they were going to be similar to his.

"Oh, Max, I...don't know what's wrong with me."

"There's nothing wrong with you." Involuntarily, his hands began to make little caressing circles against her buttocks, then he smoothed his palms up over the small of her back.

She practically purred, and that sensual, feminine sound almost made him come apart.

"Would you be mad if we . . . if I . . ."

"No." He kissed her because he'd already sensed that feminine surrender, that melting. "No," he whispered again as he broke the kiss. "I won't be mad, baby. I can guarantee that."

"Okay."

"Okay?" He had to be sure, and to defuse the moment he tried a little humor. "This will officially qualify us as eligible for a two-night stand. That's okay with you?"

"Yes." She threaded her fingers through his hair and pulled, bringing his lips up to hers. *"Please."*

Then he was lost. What was it about this woman that just a kiss reduced him to a mass of raging testosterone? He'd known that he wanted her that first evening at Swan's. What they'd shared that night had been beyond anything he'd ever experienced. Tonight he knew it would be even better, would bond them even deeper.

Perhaps that was the solution. Perhaps he simply had to make love to this woman, make love to Eve until she finally surrendered. Perhaps sex—constant, glorious, hotter-than-hot sex—was the way to bring this woman to her knees.

And that image made his blood boil.

He rolled over, taking her with him, pulling her beneath his body. He slid on top of her, pressing his body against hers. She opened her thighs, surrendered, sighed. He pushed that red silk top up, found her breasts, kissed them, licked them, took one pebbly nipple into his mouth and sucked hard until she cried out. His hand came up over her mouth, covering it gently, silencing her, but he didn't stop.

He'd never wanted a woman the way he wanted Eve. Constantly. Continually. Over and over and over again. He knew that once wouldn't be enough tonight. He wanted her with a ferocity that shocked him. It made him feel raw and untamed. Powerful.

His other hand moved between her thighs, found her hot and wet, as if she'd been ready for him all night. He touched her gently, making her moan against his hand, wanting to torment her sensually for giving him an erection that had been painful in its intensity.

He'd been wrong, he realized with the last, dim vestige of rational thought. They couldn't just sleep together. He couldn't be alone in a room without wanting to have her, over and over and over again.

Then all rational thought shorted out. Excitement and pure, raw male lust took over. He moved down her body, taking his hand away from her mouth, using both hands to part her thighs, settling his mouth there, wrenching a moan out of her, then a high, tight intake of breath. He felt her fingers in his hair, tightening, pulling, but it didn't stop him. He found her,

her heart, her heat, the wetness and scent, that part of her that promised such intense pleasure.

This time he took his time. Before, each coupling had been frenzied. Intense. Passionate. Now he was going to make it good for her, keep some sort of control, and only allow himself to go wild toward the end, once she'd been fully satisfied.

His hands moved beneath her, cupping her buttocks, guiding her as he kissed and licked and touched that most feminine part of her. He knew seconds before she climaxed. She turned her face to the side and cried out. He made her find fulfillment again before he slid up her body, against that silken, hot skin, took her wrists in his hands and pulled her to her feet.

With one hand, he swiftly pushed his pajama bottoms over his hips. They pooled at his feet and he kicked them out of the way. Max led her over to one of the chairs by the large bay window. The rain continued, but softer now, the moon offering just enough soft light so he could see her body as he unbuttoned the red silk top. He needed to see her. Looking at Eve was such a turn-on. He slid the top over her shoulders, off her body, then sat in the chair, facing her, encircling her wrists with his fingers again. He placed her so her legs straddled either side of his thighs.

"C'mere." His voice sounded rougher than he intended it to, but the sound didn't seem to scare her. He pulled her forward so her breasts pressed against his face. Taking first one nipple into his mouth, then the other, he pleasured her until he could feel her legs trembling.

"Closer." He put his hands on her hips, then guided her so that the part of her he wanted more than anything else was poised just above his strong arousal. He touched her, between her thighs, those delicate folds of skin. He opened her with his fingers and she swayed forward, her hands gripping his shoulders so tightly her fingers bit into his skin. He liked the feel of it, liked knowing she was as out of control as he was.

"Now." He grasped her hips and pushed her down on him. She moaned, then cried out as he filled her. He held her that way, perfectly still, letting her adjust to him, gritting his teeth against the strong, almost overwhelming temptation to move, to stroke her, to bring them both immediately to the most exquisite of orgasms.

"Max," she breathed, her mouth against his ear. Her voice sounded almost agonized. "Max."

He kissed her into silence, his lips and tongue playing with hers, his hands shaping her breasts. There was nothing he didn't like about her: the way she smelled, the size and shape of her breasts, the feel of her skin. It was as if she'd been designed for his pleasure, and he intended to take his fill. He felt attuned to her mood, knew she wanted this as badly as he did. He would have hoped he'd have the strength to stop if she'd asked him. He couldn't have now, not now, not when she was straddling him this way. Not when she held him so tightly inside her body.

He angled their bodies, gently, so gently, so he knew he was touching her in the best way to bring her pleasure. Then he locked his hands against the small of her back and brought her slowly up against him.

She whimpered at the intense pleasure.

"Do you like that?" he whispered.

She simply rested her head on his shoulder, her face turned away from his. A shudder ran through her body, and Max tensed. She was giving over to him, and with a woman like Eve, this moment was crucial.

"Eve," he said softly, pushing her tumbled hair away from the nape of her neck. Kissing her there. Finding the soft, delicate ear. "Eve, let me love you."

Her body trembled, her arms came up around his neck. She started to cry, and he knew he'd broken through to her, to a deeper level. He knew he'd touched her in a way those two other jerks had never even come close to doing.

He held her as she cried, stroked her back, his own pleasure forgotten as he concentrated on her. Then, as her emotions peaked and slowed, he stood. Max smiled against her hair as he felt her heels come up and lock around the small of his back. Taking his time, liking the feel of her in his arms this way, he carried her to the big bed and gently lowered her down on to her back.

He would have liked to have lit the candle, but he had a feeling Eve needed the dark right now. He was going to make sure she lost herself in pleasure. He wanted her to know how much he cared for her. He'd had a feeling tonight would bond them more closely, and he'd been right.

Max settled himself between her thighs, opening her. He pushed forward and bit his lip as he heard her sigh of pleasure. Then he pulled back, slowly, almost unsheathing himself from her and felt her fingers close around his waist, then his hips, clawing at him, bringing him back to her. He settled in then, pushing in deep, heard her moan and set to work.

It didn't take long. For either of them.

She lay very still afterward, and he watched her. Waited. When she finally stirred after almost ten minutes, he pulled her into his arms, tucked her head beneath his chin. He held her the way he'd wanted to from the first moment he'd seen her.

The storm had stopped and moonlight filled the room. Something inside his chest swelled. Threatened to break. He'd pushed her, he'd gambled, and now he wanted to win. Had to. He couldn't bear it if she tried to push him away again. He wanted this evening to be a step forward in their relationship, not backward.

He couldn't possibly put all he was feeling into words. Not yet. It was too soon, too new, too fragile.

And Eve would run like a deer caught unaware in a forest glade if he even so much as mentioned love.

So he didn't.

Max closed his eyes, lay back against the pillows. He loved the feel of Eve resting her head against his chest, and he knew she had to be able to hear how hard his heart pounded. How much their lovemaking had affected him.

He wanted her in his life. Forever. Now all he had to do was prove to her that she was safe with him.

EVE LAY AWAKE long after Max's even breathing told her he'd finally fallen asleep. The room at the Middleton Inn was perfectly silent; there were no sounds outside from either wind or rain now that the winter storm had died down.

But inside, another type of storm raged.

It seemed like a big step not to bolt out of the room a second time. She would be sharing a bed with Max until morning for the first time.

Now she could feel a sort of bond forming between them, and it scared her. Already, she felt she'd moved further emotionally in her relationship with Max than she had in either of her other two disastrous forays into love. Well, maybe they hadn't been truly disastrous, but neither of them had possessed the emotional intensity of what she had with Max.

She just didn't know what direction the relationship was supposed to go next. Having always been the logical, rational and extremely careful type, this bothered her.

She knew she wasn't skilled at this sort of thing. Eve knew she didn't have a typically daring personality, which was what made her behavior at Swan's all the more extraordinary. She'd wanted to be close to Max, she'd wanted to be sexual with him, to feel sexual again. So she had. But she'd thought it would remain within the confines of a one-night stand, never dreaming she'd have to negotiate a real relationship.

Immature, yes. Am I an emotional basket case? Right again.

She thought of distancing herself from Max, pretending to bury herself in her work. *I'll make sure I'm constantly busy, way too busy to see him—*

Stupid. Max was too sharp. He'd see right through any obvious ploy like that. Lying next to him, she knew this was the sort of relationship that could develop into something real. And it scared her. Gail had been right—when the potential for something wonderful, something real came along, it was a little overwhelming.

Okay. Do you have to decide right now? Can't you just, for once in your life, go with the flow and have a little fun? Try to be a little less anal retentive? Why not enjoy what you and Max have now and leave tomorrow to tomorrow?

It sounded good in her head. It was just hard to do in real life, with real emotions.

Finally, simply exhausted, Eve turned her face into the soft pillow and slept.

MAX SMILED into his pillow as he finally heard Eve sigh and relax. He could almost feel the struggle going on inside her head.

Eve. So beautiful, and so decidedly analytical. Layers upon layers, complicated and complex. She totally fascinated him. He knew she'd try to reason this one out, but the one thing she was going to have to face was that love was an emotion that simply couldn't always be reasoned with. And logical? Never.

Though he felt like taking her into his arms and holding her close all night, he knew she needed a little space. So he lay very still until he heard her even, rhythmic breathing, then stared at the ceiling and plotted.

All's fair, after all . . .

THE POUNDING on the door brought Eve out of an erotic dream. Starring Max, of course. She came to full consciousness to find Max in bed beside her, a finger over his lips.

"Who is it?" he called out.

"Dr. Crummond. I thought we might start early on that house-hunting expedition."

Eve looked at Max in horror, then dived beneath the covers. He got up out of bed. When she peeked out, he was shrugging on a pair of worn jeans. She pulled the covers back over her head.

"Hang on a minute," Max called.

Eve peeked again. She watched as Max checked the room for signs she was there. Her clothes were in the bathroom, she was concealed beneath the duvet. He was looking out for her, and the thought warmed her heart.

She snuggled down deeper into Max's bed.

She could tell by the sound that he only opened the door a crack.

"What's wrong, son? You look like you didn't sleep at all."

How right that observation is, Eve thought.

"The storm kept me up."

"Ahh." Eve knew Dr. Crummond's habits, and anticipated that the older man would change tactics quickly. "Well, then, do you want to go out today at all? You look like a few more hours in bed wouldn't hurt you."

"My thoughts exactly," Max said.

"Good God, we don't want you coming down with a virus or something. Got to continue your work on that new Cyber Baby. Not to mention those lectures." Now Dr. Crummond was all business.

"I know." Max coughed. "My throat has been feeling a little scratchy."

Dr. Crummond briskly made up his mind. "That's it, then. To bed with you, for the rest of the day. I'll come by tomorrow morning and we'll resume our house hunt at that time."

"I appreciate your thoughtfulness, sir."

"Any way I can be of service to you, Elliott. Just say the word and it's yours."

"Thank you, sir. You're very kind."

The door shut. Eve heard Max lock it. She waited almost ten seconds before she turned her head into the down pillow and burst into giggles.

Max slid into bed with her, beneath the duvet. He'd discarded his jeans, and his body felt cool from being out from beneath the warm covers.

"You heard what he said. I have to spend the day in bed."

She continued to laugh.

"I could end up a very sick boy if I don't follow Crummond's instructions to the letter."

She couldn't stop laughing.

Max pulled her into his arms. She caught her breath in the middle of a giggle as she felt his muscled body against her own. And discovered his arousal.

"You are terrible," she whispered. "Do you think about sex all the time?"

He pretended to consider her question. "Nah. Just ninety-eight percent of my waking hours." He kissed the tip of her nose. "But only with you."

EVE SNUCK OUT of the Middleton Inn later that afternoon, feeling like an errant teenager with Dr. Crummond as a father. Although she didn't have any real experience of what a father's supervision would be like, she imagined it would feel a lot like this.

Once at home, she stripped off her clothes, showered, then changed into comfy sweats. Though she'd planned on running a few errands, now she decided she just wanted some time to herself. Time to get her bearings.

What she had with Max was a once-in-a-lifetime experience—that kept happening over and over again. And getting better and better in the process. She could no longer pretend she didn't have feelings for him.

Eve sighed, poured herself a glass of white wine and walked into her living room. She turned one of the chairs toward the huge windows overlooking the snow-covered grove of birch trees, and sat. And stared. And sipped. And thought.

What to do?

She didn't have a whole lot of experience with men like Max. Men who were open and honest and willing to lay their feelings on the line. She knew that part of what made him such an extraordinary person was being the twin of a female. He was an incredibly sensitive male, and she knew she was lucky to have found him.

But she was scared. And she couldn't seem to make those feelings go away. She was scared Max would leave. She was scared he wouldn't leave. She was

scared he'd stay around long enough—a few years—
to have a child with her and then leave. That would
destroy her.

She knew this was about her mother, though Mary
Anne Vaughn had never made a negative reference to
Eve's father. Eve's mother had always spoken of marriage as one of life's greatest joys, and done nothing
to turn her daughter off the idea of such a union.

But nonetheless, the fears were there, and couldn't
be easily reasoned with.

Abandonment. That's what I can't get past.

Eve took a sip of wine and stared out into the cold
winter afternoon. She didn't think she'd come up with
a solution to her problems right this very minute, but
perhaps she could come up with some sort of battle
plan. That would be soothing. Comforting. Even if
she only thought she knew what she was doing, it
would be a start.

She let her mind drift, remembering their first night
at the bed and breakfast. The way Max had looked at
her as he'd first undressed her. As he'd leaned over her
on the bed. The candlelight burnishing his dark hair,
making the bedroom seem unbearably intimate. The
way his hands had felt as he'd slipped his fingers beneath her silk panties and ripped them out of the
way...

Her eyes slowly closed. She was floating in the
midst of erotic memories and getting herself quite
turned on when Eve realized someone was pounding

on her front door. And pounding as if she hadn't re-sponded to the first few knocks.

She set her wineglass down, shot up off the chair and headed toward the door.

"Eve? Are you there?"

She recognized Dr. Crummond's distinctive voice.

"Coming!" she called, wishing she'd thought to pop a breath mint. It wouldn't do for the head of her de-partment to think she'd been drinking in the middle of the afternoon. After five, it seemed that everyone in the small academic community went for a cocktail or two to relieve stress. But not before.

Composing herself, she opened the front door.

Max stood behind Dr. Crummond, looking as un-comfortable as she'd ever seen him. As Dr. Crum-mond began to speak, Max slowly shook his head and mouthed the single word "no."

"What?" Eve said, trying to understand what Max was attempting to tell her.

"What?" Dr. Crummond said, looking behind him.

"Nothing," Max replied, trying to look bland. But the expression in his dark eyes was troubled.

Dr. Crummond continued, clearly assuming Eve had heard what he'd said before.

"So you see, the Cyber Baby has arrived and our young Dr. Elliott doesn't have a place to work, a lab-oratory to call his own, if you will—"

What has this got to do with me? Eve thought wildly. She ran her fingers through her tumbled hair in an agitated manner, then stared at Max. He simply shrugged his shoulders and looked at the department head as if to say, "Just let him roll with it."

"And that finished basement of yours is ideal—"

Now she got it. It was as if she suddenly came up for air after a deep-sea dive, came to consciousness after a long sleep.

"Now, wait a minute—"

"Dr. Crummond, I don't think this is the best idea for all concerned—" Max began.

"Nonsense," Dr. Crummond said, his tone a bit huffy. It was clear he didn't like the idea of their questioning his brilliant answer to this particular dilemma. "This will be a splendid solution until we can find you a suitable house. Eve?" He gave her a look that clearly said he expected no interference from her in this matter.

She swallowed. She didn't dare look at Max. He was just as caught up in this entire mess as she was. And anyway, she knew he wasn't a man who would take unfair advantage of her.

But how was she going to stay away from him, avoid him and keep their relationship on a more even keel, if he was working out of her home?

She snapped out of her thoughts as she realized Dr. Crummond was staring at her expectantly. And expecting her to perform as a good little member of the psychology department would—if she wanted to keep her job.

"Why don't we show him the basement?" she said brightly, quietly admitting defeat.

"Lovely room," Dr. Crummond said, finishing off the last of the cheese ball and crackers. And Eve thought, not for the last time, how grateful she was she'd stocked her refrigerator for unexpected holiday guests—even if those holidays were technically over.

Max stood by one of the windows, a glass of wine in hand.

The three of them had gone downstairs to Eve's finished basement. All she really had down there was a pool table and a vintage Coke machine. In one small room off to the side she had several boxes of junk, those cardboard boxes everyone in the world has and, unopened, moves from house to house, move to move.

But other than that, she had plenty of room and had to be honest about it. Dr. Crummond was right—there was space to set up a laboratory for whatever Max might want to do.

"Dr. Elliott!" Dr. Crummond suddenly announced. "We can't keep our Dr. Vaughn away from her work a moment longer." He turned toward Eve. "Just let us know when it's convenient to bring over all the equipment."

Eve smiled, trying to soften things for Max. She had a feeling he was terribly uncomfortable about the way things had turned out, and she wanted him to know that, in her opinion, it wasn't that big a deal. What it boiled down to was that neither of them had the heart—or the nerve—to upset Dr. Crummond. Or really wanted to.

Both of them had their jobs to consider, after all.

"Anytime is fine. I'll be in all this evening, and most of the morning."

"Excellent!"

As they walked toward the front door, Eve decided to be as gracious about this whole thing as she could.

"Would you like another cheese ball, Dr. Crummond? I made several for the holidays, and I'd certainly like you to take one home to enjoy."

The department head beamed. She wrapped up the appetizer for him, along with several types of crackers, then handed him the small package. Eve watched as the two men headed toward Dr. Crummond's aging Oldsmobile. Then, before the car headed slowly down her driveway, she saw Max get out of the passenger side and come back up to her front porch.

"Don't go anywhere," he muttered, as if Dr. Crummond were standing beside him and not in the car several yards away. "I'll be back within half an hour."

She nodded her head, then watched the car disappear into the early-evening winter dusk.

Perhaps this new development warrants a new rule—no sex, and work on the friendship aspect.

But even as the thought formed in her mind, she knew she was doomed. Fate had just stepped in and given Mad Max a generous helping hand.

Life sometimes wasn't fair. And when it came to her relationship with Max she wasn't sure she wanted it to be fair.

"I DON'T KNOW what got into him," Max admitted later, over dinner. He'd come back with a pizza, and Eve had thrown together a salad and provided the wine.

"I do," Eve said, reaching for another slice of the tomato, sausage and basil pie. "He wants you to stay. He wants you to make Middleton famous. He wants you to be happy and put the psychology department on the map."

"Oh, is that all?"

The way Max said those words made her start to laugh, and he joined in. Sitting on the carpet by the coffee table, Eve leaned back against one of the chairs. Max sat across from her, against the sofa.

"He's not usually this pushy," Eve said. "In fact, he wasn't like this at all until we got wind of your coming to give your lecture series."

"That's right. Blame it all on me," Max said, but he softened his words with a smile.

"No, that's not it. I got to thinking about Dr. Crummond after the two of you left. He was a different man before his wife died. Her death changed him.

They never had any children, so I think he considers Middleton his baby. He wants to leave something behind, something good. Something that proves that he was here and his life mattered. Do you know what I mean?"

Max nodded his head. "I know. The old guy's lonely. Calls me all the time. Just to chat, as he says. Asks me all sorts of questions about the Cyber Baby. He's genuinely interested in what I'm developing, but I can tell he wants the company." His gaze on her sharpened, and Eve felt her breathing slow. There was something so compelling about Max.

"I just don't want you to think I've taken advantage of the situation," he said. "I'll find a house as soon as I can and get out of your way."

She shook her head as she took another bite of pizza, chewed, then swallowed. "No, it's okay. I know you won't take advantage. Just give me an idea of your schedule—"

"—so you can be out of the house," he finished for her.

She hesitated. "That wasn't what I was going to say."

Liar, said that little voice inside her. Straight from her gut.

Okay, maybe, but he doesn't have to know.

"I won't come into the main body of the house," Max said. "I noticed there's a second refrigerator down there, and another bathroom. I'll lock myself up down there and you won't see me until I leave in the evening."

"Max—"

"I insist. I don't want to upset your routine in any way, shape or form."

"Well, actually I was thinking about asking for the tiniest little adjustment in our relationship."

That got his attention.

"Eve?"

"I was thinking—" She cleared her throat, suddenly flustered. "Well, I was thinking that the sex is so good, so spectacular, that it's making me lose sight of everything else." She didn't like the expression beginning to form on his face. "So I thought perhaps we might give up the sex angle for a while and work on the relationship. I mean, the friendship."

"Is this what you really want?" Max asked as he slowly set down the piece of pizza he'd been holding.

She felt as if she'd come at him with a broadsword. "I think I just need to really slow things down."

He was silent for a moment before he finally spoke. "Eve, would this make you feel safer?"

What a perceptive question. What a perceptive man. "Yes. Yes, I think it would."

"Okay." He studied her for a long moment, then picked up the piece of pizza. "No sex. But I want to be clear on one thing."

"What?"

"I'd like to get back to sex as soon as possible, because it may confuse you that it's so spectacular, but it absolutely enthralls me. I'll leave it up to you, though, Eve. You let me know. I'll leave things in your hands."

"Thank you." Now, even though a part of her was relieved, she was a little disappointed she'd gotten her own way so easily. "I'll let you know."

They ate in silence for a short while, then Max spoke up.

"There's only one favor I'd like to ask."

She nodded her head, urging him to state it.

"I'd like to bring Kevin to work with me. He gets a little stir-crazy if he's left alone too long."

"That will be fine."

"And like I said, as soon as I find a house to rent, I'll move my lab elsewhere."

She simply nodded again, and wondered if she'd done the right thing.

MAX BEGAN WORK the following morning. Dr. Crummond had loaned him a large table, and now the various components of the newest Cyber Baby lay strewn out in front of him, ready to be assembled and tested.

But his mind wasn't on his work. It was on Eve.

"Kevin, what would you do?" he asked the cat.

Kevin simply sat in one of the casement windows, staring intently into the woods beyond the house. In all the time Max had owned him, Kevin had never shown any interest in being an outdoor cat. He'd had enough of the great outdoors the night Max had found him on the side of the road in the thunderstorm, soaked through. Now he was totally content to remain inside the house, out of the elements.

Which was why, when Kevin scratched at the glass and meowed, Max showed great interest.

"What is it?"

Kevin meowed louder, scratched harder.

Max walked over to the window and opened it. His fluffy comrade shot out as soon as the opening was large enough, and ran to the edge of the birches.

Max simply watched. He had no fear that Kevin had decided to run away. The cat was smart, and devoted to him. Something had caught his eye. Something that troubled him.

He returned within two minutes, a small scrap of black-and-white fur dangling from his mouth.

"Damn," Max whispered. So much for staying out of each other's way.

EVE WAS IN the kitchen, making lunch, when Max burst in.

"Do you have one of those electric room heaters?" He was cradling in his arms the most pathetic kitten she'd ever seen. Kevin brought up the rear, weaving worriedly around Max's jean-clad legs.

"Yes." She went and got it, then sat it on the kitchen floor and plugged it in. Max sat down close to it, rubbing the tiny cat with a towel from the basement bathroom, holding the damaged, defenseless animal as it shivered.

"Cat food," she said, and went to the cupboard for a small, pop-top can. She opened it, fended off both a hungry Kevin and an interested Caliban, dumped it onto a small plate and handed the plate to Max.

He put it beneath the kitten's nose. She barely sniffed it, simply curled into herself and shivered.

Max looked up at her. "Do you have a good vet?"

Eve nodded. "I'll drive."

YOU HAD TO BE impressed, Eve thought, by a man who was willing to spend over a hundred dollars on a scrap of fur he hadn't even known existed this morning. The kitten had been given fluids, nutrients and antibiotics, had been put in a heated incubator and would be watched round the clock by the staff at the animal hospital.

"Someone clearly abandoned this little one in the woods," the vet had told them. "Perhaps a kitten that didn't behave the way this person thought it should. Or the last of a litter they couldn't find a home for. In any case, this little runt's been on her own for quite some time. She's very thin."

"Whatever it takes," Max had told the doctor. She'd smiled up at him, clearly as impressed as Eve was.

Now they were back in Eve's kitchen and sitting at her table.

"I was just heating up some leftover stew for lunch," she said. "Would you like some?"

"If you're sure."

"It won't take a minute."

He washed up while she set the table and dished out the hot stew. Bread and apple juice from a local orchard rounded out their meal.

"This is very nice," Max remarked when he was halfway through lunch.

"What you did was very nice. What Kevin did was extraordinary."

"He's a terrific cat. It cost him a lot to go back outside. He's terrified to be out of the house." Max reached for another slice of bread. "But he must have seen, or sensed, that kitten in distress and wanted to help."

"What a cat."

Max leaned back in his chair. "And an incredible show of compassion. I'm always amazed by the things animals do for each other. By what humans choose to do for each other. The media tends to play up our worst actions, you see so much negativity on the news. But for each bit of evil in the world I believe there are countless acts of generosity."

He fascinated her, the way his mind worked. "Will you touch on this in your lectures?"

He smiled. "That philosophy is at the core of almost everything I do."

Eve could feel her heart race. Why had she insisted on that stupid no-sex-work-on-the-friendship rule? It seemed that every time she thought she had a handle on Max, he went and did something that made her like him even more.

If he could be this kind to a defenseless kitten abandoned out in the snow, he would be nothing but magnificent with the woman he loved, a sneaky little voice inside her insisted.

But you're not even that sure of how he feels about you, another more cautious voice insisted, playing devil's advocate. *So far, it's been spectacular sex, and that can cloud rational thinking. Hormones have been known to make people do crazy things.*

So Eve merely smiled at Max and poured him more apple juice. One thing she was going to give herself in this relationship was time. And just the tiniest bit of hope.

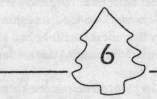

6

"HAVE YOU SEEN HIM?" the young, feminine voice whispered.

Eve, one aisle over in the campus bookstore, didn't even have to hear a name to know which visiting professor these two students were discussing.

"Oh, God, I'm not going to miss one of his lectures. He can talk to me about the mating ritual between male and female Homo sapiens any day of the week."

"Or night," the other added, and they both laughed.

Eve turned away and walked down another aisle in the crowded college bookstore. One of her texts hadn't arrived on time, and she was double-checking to make sure it was in today, Friday, the first official day of second semester. Though there were no classes until Monday morning, if her students could stop by sometime over the weekend and pick up this one last textbook, they wouldn't fall too far behind in their reading.

But the big news on campus didn't have anything to do with textbooks. It had to do with Dr. Alexander Maximillian Elliott, the inventor of the Cyber

Baby. She'd seen the poster for his lecture series up by the front door, which included a photo of Max, dressed in jeans and a denim shirt. The bookstore manager had blithely informed Eve that several had been stolen and now had places of honor in female dorm rooms.

Eve had a feeling that this was one series of lectures that was going to have an extraordinarily high turn-out—but for all the wrong reasons. You'd have thought that Elvis himself had risen from the dead, the way students were reacting.

Eve headed out the door, fastening her beige down coat against the cold January wind. Some things never changed. College students would always be over-loaded with hormones, and operating primarily from that biological level.

You haven't been doing so badly yourself recently, that mischievous little voice whispered.

Oh, shut up.

She didn't want to think about Max. Since the in-cident with the kitten, now named Harley for her loud purr and firmly ensconced as Kevin's playmate, Max had been on her mind constantly. Though he was completely isolated in her basement and she made a point of leaving him alone with his inventions, she couldn't stop thinking about the man.

Her own no-sex rule was driving her crazy. Typical reverse psychology. Now that she couldn't have sex with Max, it was all she thought about. And she had a sneaking little suspicion that he knew it.

Max arrived at eight each morning, and left promptly at seven each night. He never subtly invited himself to dinner, or finagled his way into other parts of her life. The most he'd done was to leave the door at the top of the stairs open so Caliban could come down into the basement and play with Harley, who fascinated him. Kevin and Caliban still gave each other a wide, respectful distance.

She knew he had a house and that it was almost ready for him to move into. It was farther up the hill, close to Dr. Crummond's. All his lab equipment had arrived, but his personal possessions had been delayed because of severe snowstorms farther west. But Mad Max, as he was beginning to be called on the small, liberal arts campus, didn't let that faze him.

She knew he had all the notes for his lecture series. He'd packed them with his lab material. Sometimes, when he stayed late at night, she heard him clicking away on his laptop computer, integrating new material into his talks. He worked constantly, with a strong sense of discipline. Eve admired that. But there were times when she wondered if he even knew she was alive.

HE THOUGHT ABOUT HER constantly.

This no-sex rule is going to kill me.

It wasn't that he only wanted her that way. He liked all of Eve. Her mind, her heart . . . and yes, her body. Max sighed, then got up from his chair and walked over to the basement window. Gazing out at the birches, he wondered if Eve would ever trust him enough to let him into her world.

He understood much more than she thought he did. Her fears and vulnerabilities. He'd seen firsthand, and on an extremely emotional level, what casual cruelty and total abandonment could do to a woman's soul. With Annie. While his twin sister hadn't been punished for getting pregnant at the age of sixteen, it had been clear that their father hadn't been happy with this particular twist in Annie's life. Their mother had been the peacemaker, but the months before Annie gave birth to her stillborn child had been tense.

His bedroom had been next to hers. And in the way of most twins, they'd had a link. Many nights, when he'd pretended to be reading in bed, he'd heard soft sobs coming from the direction of her dark bedroom. Max had told her he was there for her, anytime, any-place. But there were some pains so private they had to be faced alone.

He'd been with her right after her little boy had been born, so tiny and still, and it had been the most ter-rifying time of his life. He'd thought he was going to lose his sister, and he couldn't imagine a life without her. They'd always been so close.

He'd watched as Annie had made valiant attempts to come out of her grief, then tried to shed the careful shell she'd erected around her emotions. And that had taken time, even with the support of a loving family. A mother and father who adored her, an older brother, Graham, who cherished her, and a twin who thought the world of her.

She hadn't dated again until she was almost twenty. Three long years. She'd hidden at home, finished her high school diploma privately, then taken their father's advice and signed up for a year in France. A cooking school. Something totally different, something to jump-start her life.

And she'd met Jacques.

Max had known, the moment he'd met the tall, dark, volatile Frenchman, that he was the one for Annie. But it had taken Annie a little time to get used to the idea. She'd been comfortable with her heart hidden away, and didn't ever want to be hurt again. But Jacques had been persistent, and now they were happily married and the proud parents of three beautiful children—and planning on a fourth. Annie was a natural mother, and watching her with her children always made Max feel like all was right in the world.

Now, here at Middleton University, Eve's fears reminded him so much of what his twin had gone through.

Maybe you did rush into sex too soon. He was willing to admit it. Maybe it had all been too much for

Eve to handle, and now she needed this retreat of sorts. Well, he could take it. He could be a patient man. He could wait for a woman as special as Eve.

In all of his experience with women, he'd never met anyone like her. So prickly, so sharp, then that total melting, that sweet giving over. That incredible intensity.

Max realized he was staring blindly out at the grove of birch trees, so he walked away from the window. Eve had supplied him with an electric heater, which he kept plugged in by his desk. Currently, Kevin was lying in front of it, a reluctant and fluffy Harley pinned beneath one of his massive paws as he proceeded to give her a thorough bath with his rough pink tongue.

"And they say the male of the species has no maternal instincts," Max muttered, then smiled. He glanced up as a movement caught his eye, and saw Caliban at the top of the basement stairs, peering down.

"Come on," he said softly, letting the little black cat know he was welcome.

Caliban hesitated, then slowly came down about three steps. He stopped. Sat. Regrouped.

Like Eve, Max thought. *So cautious.* He stretched, rotated the tired kinks out of his shoulders, then walked back to his desk and sat down. Thinking about Eve wasn't going to get the newest model of his Cyber Baby finished. Since he had to give her time to get used to the idea of having a man in her life, that time could certainly be put to better use than daydreaming. Because, even though they were in the same house, for the moment, Eve was as out of his reach as if she lived on the moon.

"COFFEE?" Patty asked as Eve walked up to the main counter of The Brew-Ha-Ha.

"I'd like—what's the one with all the milk called?"

"Latte. You okay? You seem a little out of sorts."

"I'm okay."

Patty hesitated. "How about a mocha latte? A little bit of chocolate never hurts on a day like this."

"Sounds good."

The coffeehouse was busy this morning, with students returning from vacation and meeting up with each other. Eager young voices could be heard discussing what they'd done on vacation, classes they were planning to take and what they wanted to do once spring break came around. Looking out the window at the high drifts of snow and the leaden Ohio sky, Eve could understand why anyone would want to think of sunnier parts of the country.

"Want some company?" Patty asked as she brought Eve's mocha latte to the small table by one of the front windows.

"I'd love some."

"Good. I'll take my break. Just let me get some coffee and I'll be right back."

Eve sipped her coffee. Patty had been right; chocolate improved any mood. Her friend joined her within minutes, carrying her own coffee and a colorful plate heaped with biscotti, muffins and croissants.

"Trying to make me fat," Eve accused.

"Trying to get your blood sugar up and get you in a better mood. You look like someone just ran over your dog."

"I'm that transparent?"

"To me you are. Want to talk?"

Eve considered this option, then nodded her head. She and Patty had always used a kind of emotional shorthand. She'd never hesitated to confide in her friend.

"Max."

"Hmm."

"I think I'm in love with him."

Patty smiled. "Good choice."

"But . . . I'm scared."

"Of course you are."

Eve stared at her.

"You're scared because a lot of men choose not to stick around, including your own father. So you think the same thing is going to happen with Max, but I can tell you that it won't. I'm one hundred percent sure."

"How can you know that?"

"Because he came in here one afternoon. And we talked about you. He got straight to the point. Eve, the man's nuts about you. He's got it bad. He wants you, and I think you should toss caution to the wind and go for it."

"I wish I were that brave."

"You can be."

"Should I just tell him?"

Patty sighed, then leaned forward, breaking off part of a blueberry-cinnamon muffin. "Max is the sort of man you can tell anything to. Don't you think?"

Eve considered this, then changed the subject. "What did you tell him? About me?"

"A little family-of-origin stuff. I told him not to be mad at you if it took a little time, because you definitely had your reasons for being cautious. I hope you're not angry at me, Eve. I only did it because I want you two to make it."

"No." She stared down at the large mug, then took another sip of coffee. "I'm not angry."

"Look," Patty said, sliding the plate toward Eve, encouraging her to make a choice. "It's Friday, everyone's just returned and classes won't begin until Monday morning. If I know you, you had your lesson plans completed ages ago. Why don't you go back to your house, grab Max out of that basement and tell him you want to go away with him for the weekend? That way, the two of you can interact without everyone on campus being able to observe."

"That has kind of held me back. That's part of it," Eve admitted, reaching for an almond biscotti. "I don't like the way people gossip on this small a campus. And I would never want to do anything that would hurt Max."

"It wouldn't hurt Max—he'd rise above it. And it would probably give you added status on campus. After all, Crummond would think you were going all out to keep Max here at Middleton."

"Patty!" But Eve laughed.

"Talk to Max. Tell him you want a relationship with him, but you have to go slow. Encourage the poor guy, don't let him feel like you're rejecting him—"

"I wouldn't want to do that."

"Exactly. But men, even men like Max, can be fairly dense. They need a little reassurance once in a while, just like we do."

"You really think I should do this?"

Patty nodded her head. "I do. I don't want to see a great guy like Max get discouraged and decide to go for another, lesser woman on this campus."

"Good point." Eve hadn't wanted to entertain that possibility. She finished her coffee, set the mug down, studied her friend. "Not to change the subject, but did you color your hair or gain weight or something? You look fabulous."

Patty's blue eyes glowed with happiness. "I think being pregnant might have a little bit to do with it."

It took a few seconds for the news to hit Eve.

"Patty!" Eve knew of her friend's longing for a child, of the three miscarriages she'd been through. "Oh,

Patty, this is wonderful!" Inside, she worried, but she would give her friend nothing but support.

"I'm past the first trimester, so this time I'm going to make it—"

Eve watched as her friend's eyes filled with tears.

"I just told Glen the other night. He was happy, Eve, but—"

"What?" Now Eve reached across the table and took Patty's hand in hers. It felt so fine boned and delicate.

"I think he's . . . afraid to hope again."

Eve considered this. She'd worked with Glen for several years, and thought he was a terrific man, and a supportive husband.

"I think he's afraid for you."

"You think so? I hadn't thought of that. Well, he doesn't have to be, 'cause this time nothing's going to go wrong." Patty blinked away her tears, then sniffed. She reached for a napkin. "I can feel it."

I hope you're right. Eve had been at the hospital the last time Patty had miscarried. She would carry the picture of Glen's agonized face in her memory for the rest of her life.

"I know you're right, Patty." She couldn't possibly voice her own doubts to her friend. Not at this time. It would have been unspeakably selfish. "You look just beautiful." She frowned. "Should you be working this hard?"

Patty laughed as she gestured around the coffee shop with her hands. "You and Glen! Two mother hens. I'm fine, Eve. I'm just worried about you and Max. Now tell me what you're going to do."

"I'm going back to his lab and coming clean. If we leave tonight, we'll have two nights off campus with each other. We can get a lot resolved in that time."

Patty took her hand. "Resolve what you have to, but don't get so nervous you forget to have fun. I'll bet Max is a really fun guy."

If you only knew. "I'll remember that."

"And Eve . . . ?"

"Yes."

"You don't have to sleep with him. You can book separate rooms. This is the nineties, after all."

"I'll consider that." Then, squeezing Patty's hand, Eve felt her eyes sting. "I'm so happy for you."

"Thanks."

"How did you...how did you decide to...after..." She couldn't quite articulate what she was feeling.

Patty patted Eve's restlessly drumming fingers with her other hand. "Sometimes you just have to take a leap of faith." She smiled. "Keep that in mind, Eve."

"MAX, COULD I TALK to you for a minute?"

He sat up straighter the second he heard Eve's voice at the top of the stairs.

"Sure. Come on down."

Kevin and Caliban were chasing a delighted Harley round and round the pool table. The fluffy black-and-white kitten had fully regained her strength, and was now overstimulated from her joyful exertions.

Max watched as Eve came down the stairs. She was dressed in a long, camel-colored wool skirt, brown leather boots and a multicolored sweater in various earth tones. On her, it looked fabulous. He thought about getting up from behind his desk, bending her over the pool table, lifting that sweater over her head, unsnapping her bra, slipping off that skirt—

"Max, I'd like to go away with you for the weekend."

That got his attention.

"Eve?"

She cleared her throat, and he could tell she was nervous. "I'd like to get away from this campus until late Sunday night. I'd like to go somewhere where we can have some privacy and time to...get to know each other better."

"Okay." He was deliberately reticent, sensing that if he made one wrong move she might bolt like a frightened deer. "Do you want me to book us separate rooms?"

She took a deep breath. "No."

His world rocked, but he forced himself to remain calm.

"Can you be ready to leave within the hour?"

He smiled. "You bet."

HE MADE ONE necessary phone call before picking her up in his Porsche. To Swan's Bed and Breakfast. Max wanted everything to go perfectly this weekend, and would do whatever it took to accomplish that aim.

Eve called one of her students to house-sit, and arranged for her to look after Caliban, Kevin and Harley for the weekend.

They drove swiftly off campus, away from the rolling hills it had been built on, to the interstate below. Then Max sped up, and drove as swiftly as was safe. The weather was excellent for a road trip—cold, crisp and clear. Snow flurries weren't expected until early next week.

He glanced over at her. Eve, who had been looking out the window at the passing scenery, at everything but him, had nodded off. Max smiled. He understood. He could almost sense the tension coiled up inside her. She was the sort of woman who would work at having a good time. Who didn't laugh a lot. Who was almost heartbreakingly cautious.

As he drove, Max resolved to make sure she had a lot of fun this weekend.

THEY CHECKED IN at just past one in the afternoon, to the same room they'd shared last time, then went downstairs and had lunch in the bed and breakfast's small dining room. Eve ordered the chicken pot pie, while Max had fish and chips. Then they retired to their room.

"Would you rather have booked separate rooms?" Max asked her as he locked the door behind them.

"No," she said quietly.

He was trying to gauge her mood and not succeeding very well. She'd been quiet the entire drive. Now he wasn't quite sure how to handle things, but decided to go with his gut.

Eve always opened up a little more after they'd been intimate. He'd go for that kind of communication, and unless his instincts were completely wrong, she wanted what he wanted as badly as he did.

He hadn't slept with her since that evening at the Middleton Inn, the night of the thunderstorm. Max hadn't thought it wise to insist on continuing that part of their relationship, especially as Eve had changed the rules, slowed things down. Now he hoped she'd missed their physical intimacy as much as he had.

He couldn't be sure. But he'd try. Keeping his attention on her, he dialed the front desk.

"Hello? I'd like to request that we're not disturbed until dinner. Thank you."

He'd guessed right. Her eyelids lowered, her eyes darkened. The look she gave him indicated, to him, that her thoughts were heading in the same direction as his were. When she'd said she wanted time alone with him, their physical relationship had been part of that request.

Max walked over toward the large bed. Reached into his bag. Took out a package.

"For you." He handed it to her. She seemed delighted as she tore off the paper, then laughed as she examined the contents of the package.

The red silk pajama top.

He'd enclosed a note. "This looks far better on you than it ever will on me. Max."

She laughed, then carefully laid the red silk garment on one of the pillows. She turned toward him. Looked up at him.

"Eve?" Now he was asking permission. He didn't want to go too fast, didn't want to frighten her. "What would you like?" he whispered.

"Would you . . . would you take the decision out of my hands one more time?" She seemed almost in a wistful mood, and it charmed him.

This he knew he could do. He brought her hand up to his lips, kissed her fingertips.

"I thought you'd never ask."

SHE WANTED HIM to make love to her. Though she knew he'd been simply following her wishes, Eve had been frustrated at not being with Max. Now, lying next to him in bed was like a drug, the scent of him, the warmth he radiated.

He kissed her fingertips, one by one, and she melted. During sexual encounters in the past, she'd thought there was something wrong with her because she couldn't respond. But, with Max, she'd begun to get aroused as soon as he agreed to join her for the weekend. As she gazed out the window of Max's car, she'd thought about what could happen this weekend, and had gotten turned on.

He kissed her mouth, and she leaned against him, let him support her. He wasn't greedy, simply cajoling, urging her on, opening her mouth, sliding his tongue inside. Then he deepened the kiss, making it unbearably intimate and erotic.

She whimpered against his mouth, then sighed as she felt him reach down, lift her off her feet. Soon she would feel the bed against her back, they'd take off their clothes and—

He set her down facing the back of one of the chairs by the large bay window. Sheer drapes covered the glass, the heavier drapes still pulled aside. Outside, the sky had clouded up. Inside, with the heater turned up high, they were in a warm, private world of their own.

"Max?" She looked back over her shoulder at him.

"Would you indulge me?" He lifted her hair up off the nape of her neck and kissed her there.

She wondered what it was he wanted, and her expression must have revealed her thoughts to him.

He looked utterly unrepentant. "When you came down the basement stairs this afternoon, when you started talking to me, I had this incredible sexual fantasy."

She was instantly intrigued. Max, Mad Max, Max the scientist, made everything sexual seem plausible.

"Go on."

"I wanted to bend you over the pool table, lift up your skirt and just have you that way. Not even wait to get naked. Not take too much time before getting right to it."

She could feel her body catching fire at his words. The sound of his voice, the images he conjured up for her, made her want the same thing he did.

"Yes," she whispered.

"What are you wearing?" he asked.

She turned to face him, then slowly lifted the long, wool skirt. Up past her thigh-high stay-up nylons, up to the small wisp of black lace panties. Eve watched his face the entire time, and she wasn't disappointed.

He moved closer, slid his hands beneath her skirt, rested them on her hips, then slid them over her buttocks, then beneath the black lace. Caressing her. Pulling her against him as he kissed her. Deepened the kiss.

She could only grasp his shirtfront, then slip her hands up around his neck, and hold on. His kisses made her quiver. When his hand slipped around to the front of her panties and his fingers slid beneath the elastic to the hot, wet heart of her, her head fell back and she moaned.

"Do you want me, Eve?"

She barely managed to say the word.

"*Yes....*"

He caught hold of her hand; then she realized he'd unfastened his jeans when her hand was pressed against his erection. Her fingers closed around the strong, proud flesh.

"Can you feel how much I want you?" he whispered against her ear.

She couldn't talk, simply started to slide her fingers up and down the hotly engorged length. He let her, all the while easing her panties down until they slipped to her booted feet. She stepped out of the black lace.

His kisses grew rougher. "Take off your skirt."

She looked up at him. "I thought—"

"I'd like you a little more naked."

His words, his absolute command of the situation, excited her. And for the first time, standing in a private room, all alone with Max, with no chance of their being interrupted, with no chance of anyone stopping them, she began to feel her power. Not a power to dominate, but a power to pleasure. A totally feminine power to make him feel. To carry him to his utmost pleasure.

She let go of his arousal. Found the skirt's zipper. Slid it down. Let the garment fall to the carpeted floor and kicked it away. She resisted the urge to cover herself when she saw the heat in his eyes. And she knew that for Max, visual stimulation intensified the experience.

"The sweater," he whispered.

Perhaps he wanted her completely naked while he remained dressed. Eve didn't care. Max did for her what no other man ever could or would. Each time they came together physically, she was transported into another world, where only sensation mattered.

She slowly peeled the sweater over her head. When she saw the expression in Max's eyes, she was glad she'd chosen to wear her black lace bra.

Without his needing to say a word, she slowly reached for the front fastening of her bra, then slid it open. She didn't take it off just yet, simply let one of the straps fall down her shoulder. She looked up at him. Smiled. Then slowly, her eyes never leaving his, she removed the scanty piece of lingerie.

"Turn around," he whispered.

She did, bracing herself against the back of the chair. He came up behind her, stood between her spread legs, then positioned himself for that ultimate joining. She felt him against her, hot and hard and ready; then he was sliding inside her and she was almost ashamed at how ready she was for him.

Almost. But not quite.

She moaned. He moved. Filled her. Quickly. Sharply. And she knew this was a purely male fantasy, that Max wanted her on a very primitive level. It would be hot, and urgent, and erotic. He would take what he wanted from her, and in the process give her pleasure she'd never even dreamed of.

She bit her lip against a moan as he cupped her breasts, then couldn't stop the soft whimpers that escaped. What he was doing to her just felt too good.

They didn't talk, didn't kiss, simply escalated sensation until she felt herself on that brink, felt that hot burning where their bodies were joined, felt that sense of inevitability. . . .

At precisely the right moment, Max reached down and caressed her where they came together, at that most sensitive part that craved his touch.

She shattered.

He followed her, mere seconds later, thrusting strongly in and out of her satiated, willing body. When they were finished, she couldn't even stand. He carried her to bed, stripped off her nylons and boots, then slid beneath the duvet and cradled her in his arms until she fell asleep.

"MAX?"

"Hmm?"

She could hear the smile in his voice.

"I was going to ask if you were awake, but you obviously are."

He laughed. "A little more than awake."

A quick brush against his hard, muscled body told her exactly just how awake he was.

"Max!" But she laughed, loving the idea that simply being in bed with her could arouse him this way. In some ways, he was a very uncomplicated man.

"Just before I fell asleep," he said, his voice soft against her ear, "I was thinking, 'I'm sure glad we got right to it.'"

"I know what you mean," she said.

"It kind of helps break the tension between us."

"You feel kind of tense." She closed her fingers around his erection and was rewarded by his sharp intake of breath.

"Just because... it's there, you don't have to feel... compelled to do anything with it."

She loved the fact that he was fighting for control.

"Oh, I don't know. Why let something this good go to waste?"

"You little tease." His eyes were affectionate as he looked at her.

"Only with you."

"I hope so."

She liked that hint of male possessiveness.

"What now?" she whispered.

"What would you like?"

"Oh, Max." She snuggled next to him, slid her arms around his neck, pressed her body against his. Why was it that here in bed, she felt none of the fear that would claim her later? Why was it that their sexual relationship felt good and right and complete? But when thoughts about the future, about their relationship facing the real world, intruded into her consciousness, she began to have doubts.

It was only when she thought of Max leaving her that she became afraid.

"Such a frown," he said softly, kissing her forehead. "Want to tell me about it?"

"Nope." She resumed stroking his arousal. "But there is something you could do for me. Right now."

"Anything."

She moved so her lips were against his ear. "Ravish me, Max," she whispered.

He rolled them over so he was suddenly on top of her, cradled between her thighs. Then he slid his hands down her back, cupped her buttocks and began to ease slowly inside her. She closed her eyes, in total ecstasy.

"With pleasure," he whispered as he filled her completely, then began to move. "With pleasure."

7

THE SHARP RAPPING at the door intruded on the silence inside, breaking into Eve's warm cocoon of sensual pleasure.

"Oh, no," she muttered from beneath the duvet. She'd still been in a daze from their recent lovemaking but now reached for Max's muscled back. "It can't be Crummond, can it?"

He started to laugh as he reached for his jeans. "I don't think so. It's dinner."

"Dinner?"

"I arranged to have it sent up."

The knock sounded again, and Eve simply burrowed deeper beneath the covers. Max answered the door. She heard the conversation between him and one of the waiters, then the slight squeak of a wheeled tray. The door shut again.

She peeked out from beneath the duvet. Tantalizing aromas filled the air.

"Max." She felt as if she had to be glowing with pleasure. "This is so . . . sweet."

He smiled at her. "I have my motives. This way, we don't have to get dressed." He was already shedding his jeans.

"Shouldn't we put something on . . . I mean, when we eat dinner . . . ?"

"Indulge me," he said.

She studied him, a mock-stern expression on her face. "That's two fantasies you've indulged yourself in this weekend. So far. And we're not even to Saturday."

His face was angelically bland. She wanted to laugh.

"You're keeping count?"

"Well, no. I guess that's what this weekend is for."

"Anytime you want a fantasy indulged, Eve, just let me know."

"I'll think about that."

IT WAS UTTERLY DECADENT, eating dinner in the nude. But strangely enough, with Max, it just seemed normal.

"I've never been able to make a béarnaise sauce this good," Eve said, polishing off the last of her vegetables.

"You wouldn't have to cook for the rest of your life, if you just ate dinner naked every night." He grinned.

"Max!" She blushed, then looked away.

"I love the way you do that, the way the color starts at your breasts and just travels up . . ." His voice trailed off, and she knew, without looking at him, that he was following that trail of bright color with his eyes.

And it was turning her on.

"What's for dessert?" she asked, wanting to change the subject.

"I just told them to send up whichever dessert had the most whipped cream."

Now she really blushed, could feel her face flame.

"Max. You're a bad boy."

"Nah. Just adventurous." He caught her eye. "Would you indulge me one more time?"

She felt adventurous, as well. "I'll indulge you as many times as you want to be indulged."

"I'll remember that. Okay, get down on the floor."

"Max!"

"You said you'd indulge me."

She did. He'd lit the fire, and now she lay down on the thick rug in front of the fireplace, the warmth from the flames helping her to relax. Still, Eve was a little anxious. What did Max have planned for her?

"Max?" she said.

"Eve, would you trust me if I asked you to do something?"

She turned her head so she could see his face. He had the covered dessert dish in his hands, and was walking toward her. As usual, the sight of his muscled, masculine body almost took her breath away. He always seemed to make her feel light-headed. While Max seemed perfectly civilized at the university or in other public places, when they were alone like this, he was a primitive male animal, intent on getting what he wanted.

And he had quite an appetite for pleasure.

"What do you want me to do?"

He set the dessert down close to her, then went to his suitcase and withdrew a large square of red silk.

"It came with the pajamas," he said.

She was beginning to get his drift.

"You want to . . . tie me up."

"Not yet."

Not yet. This man was outrageous. But she liked his boldness.

Max smiled down at her. "I'd like to blindfold you. I've been told it heightens sensation."

"I've been told! Like you've never been blindfolded before."

"Never have. But you can do anything you want with me. As I said before, this body is mere putty in your hands."

She couldn't help laughing. And she was getting a little aroused, at the thought of Max taking control this way.

"Okay," she said.

"Okay?"

"Yeah."

"Trust me?"

"I do," she whispered.

He studied her, standing in front of her as she lay on her back on the thick rug. "This could get a bit messy. I'd better get a towel."

She smiled as he left for the bathroom. "So you've got this all worked out in your head."

"Oh, Eve, I think about you all the time."

That got her going. She sat up as he spread the large bath sheet by the fire, then lay back down on the soft, terry surface.

"Okay." Now she felt truly adventurous. "Do with me what you will."

He knelt down, kissed her on the mouth—a long, hard kiss. "Thank you, Eve. I know it can't be easy for you."

"The crazy thing is, with you, it is."

That pleased him. "Good."

Then she stopped talking as he ran the red silk through his fingers, shaped it into a blindfold and tied it around her head.

She couldn't see, and could instantly tell her other senses were heightened. Eve didn't know what to expect, and that sensual anticipation aroused her even further.

"Lie back down."

Oh, that voice. She did as she was told.

She heard rummaging.

"What are you doing?" she whispered.

"Just a few more surprises."

She liked the way his mind worked.

Eve knew the instant he knelt down beside her.

"Whipped cream all over my body, right?"

He kissed her. Slowly. Seductively. "Oh, no. That would be rushing things. I'm going to take things very slowly with you tonight, Eve. I want you to be happy."

"Hmm." She was, after kissing him like that.

"If you don't like anything, just tell me to stop. I give you my word."

"Okay." She felt perfectly safe with him, but still there was that edge. The unknown. Uncertainty.

"Lie back. Relax. Arms above your head."

She did as she was told.

Noises. She couldn't identify them. Then she felt Max's palms come down over her stomach, slick with warm oil.

A massage. Her breath caught. How lovely.

And this man knew what he was doing. His oiled palms kneaded and shaped her body, slowly working all the tension from her shoulders and arms, her breasts and belly, then lower. Her thighs, her legs, but never touching where she wanted him to. . . .

The oil felt wonderful, light and vanilla scented. She drifted into contentment, on that towel by the fire, letting him touch her body, feel her.

"Turn over."

Now he did her back, her spine, all the way down. The back of her neck. Eve felt all tension leaving her in a wonderful, sensual rush. He kneaded her buttocks, slid his hands over her hips, down her legs, then to her feet, where he pressed and rubbed until she almost cried out in delight.

Nothing had ever made her feel so pampered.

"Stay still," he whispered, and she wondered what he was going to do next.

She felt something warm dripping down her back.

She smelled it. Hot fudge sauce. Actually, comfortably warm fudge sauce.

"Mmm." She didn't say anything more than that, until Max began to slowly lick his way up her spine. She almost came up off the towel.

"Just lie still."

"You have . . ." she said, fighting for breath as his tongue did the most sensually tortuous things to her, "the most inventive mind of anyone I've ever met."

"I'm a scientist," he whispered, and she could hear the repressed laughter in his voice. "We look for all the possibilities."

She didn't think she could stand much more. Eve was so ready for Max, she thought she might embarrass herself by climaxing right there. But she didn't; she bit her lip and held on to her control until he gently turned her over on her back.

"Hot fudge sundaes?" she whispered.

He kissed her again, and she could taste the rich, sweet chocolate sauce. "Don't talk. I only want you to feel."

"Oh . . ."

Then she felt the coolness of whipped cream. He was dolloping it liberally on her breasts, and she almost came up off the towel again.

"Max!"

"Shh." He soothed her to silence, then held her still as he licked the cream off her breasts, paying extra attention to each nipple. They hardened instantly, and Eve moaned as he gave first one, then the other, expert attention. Slowly. Soothingly. Max wasn't one to rush anything this intimate, and now she was in sensual agony.

She couldn't stand it.

"Touch me," she whispered.

"Where?"

"Please . . ."

He didn't, simply continued to caress her with his mouth, his hands, until she felt she'd go mad.

"Where?" he whispered against her ear. "Show me."

She took his hand. Guided it. Pressed it against the juncture of her thighs. She was so aroused, so wet, it amazed even her. He'd reduced her to a mindless, quivering mass of need, and all she knew was that he had to give her what she wanted, he had to give her relief from this unbearable, sensual bondage.

Her breath caught in her throat as he slipped one finger inside.

"Here?" he whispered.

"Yes!" She moved against him, her hips undulating, wanting. Taking. He soothed her with that finger, and when he slipped in a second, she cried out.

"Tell me what you want."

She continued to move against that maddening hand. Blindfolded, all sensation was captured between her thighs, those feelings were all she could think about, all she could feel.

"I want...I want..." She was almost there, she had to get there, she—

He slipped away. Maddening.

"Max!"

He was back in an instant, this time with another, smaller towel. He rubbed it all over her body, and though a part of her knew he was going to take her to their big bed and had to make sure any excess oil wouldn't stain the sheets, the feel of that nubby, cotton towel all over her aroused body was heightening sensation to almost unbearable limits.

It slipped between her breasts and she almost screamed, almost grabbed it out of his hands, she was that much out of control. She heard him toss it, then he caught her up in his arms and carried her toward the bed. She caught back a sob, she wanted him so badly; she'd never wanted anything so badly.

He came down over her on the big bed and she groaned, then pressed up against his hot, hard body.

"Please, Max. *Please* ..."

She wanted him inside her, but he had other plans, sliding down her body, spreading her thighs apart, lowering his head and taking her with his mouth. She did scream then, and his hand came up, covering her mouth as she climaxed, the release painful in its intensity.

Eve was still recovering from her climax when she felt his fingers take her arms, then felt a piece of satin material being tied around her wrists.

"Max?" Her voice sounded tentative to her ears.

"The pajamas came with a robe. This is the tie. Do you mind?"

She couldn't have really stopped him if she did. She felt boneless, her muscles didn't seem to want to work. She could barely form a coherent sentence.

"Eve?" He'd stopped now.

She smiled. She liked this new side of Max, these sensual games. He was a daring man in bed. Curious. Willing to try anything. He'd push her to new limits, and she found she liked those limits. Correction. She didn't want *any* sexual limits between them....

"No. Go on." Somehow, in the depths of feminine wisdom, she knew what he wanted, needed to hear. "I'm completely yours."

In the brief pause that followed she could sense his reaction to her words.

He finished tying her wrists, not tight enough to hurt her but definitely tight enough to restrain her.

"Does this mean," she whispered, "that I get to tie you up sometimes?"

"You can do whatever you want to do to me."

"Putty," she muttered.

He laughed, then mounted her, slid between her thighs. She sighed.

"This," she whispered, "has something to do with the biological male need to totally conquer."

"Yep." He kissed her. She melted. "Do you like being conquered?"

"More than I ever thought possible," she admitted. "What happens next?"

"Whatever you want. You tell me what you want."

She whispered words to him that were shocking in their explicitness, but seemed exactly right for where both of them were right now. The blindfold seemed like a mask, and it felt as if another side of her were coming out from behind it.

And he complied.

He felt huge and hot as he slid into her body, so deeply, so completely, and Eve whimpered in response. This was what she'd been waiting for, from the moment he'd first tied on that red silk blindfold. Now, unable to see and with restricted movement, she could only open herself to him, give him what he wanted.

Now he wasn't carefully restrained with his movements. Now he wasn't in control. Now he was simply a man who was single-mindedly in pursuit of sensation.

She reached that peak seconds before he did. Almost at the same time. Eve felt him climax, her arms straining instinctively to embrace him, to pull him closer.

They lay afterward for long moments, until she felt him lever himself up from her, taking his weight on his elbows. He untied the blindfold and she looked up into his eyes.

"Max," she whispered, just before he kissed her. "That was wonderful."

He grinned, then started to untie her hands.

"I have just one little request."

"Okay."

"I think I have some ideas concerning a little fantasy of my own. That is, if you're up to it."

His eyes darkened at the challenge. "I'm up to it."

She scrambled to her knees. "Okay. Where's that chocolate sauce?"

Now he looked worried.

"You're not going to back out on me now, are you?" Eve knew they were exactly the right words to choose. No man could resist a challenge.

"No."

"Hand me that blindfold."

He was enjoying her new independence, she could tell. As gently as she could, she blindfolded him.

"Now where was that sash?"

He started to laugh.

Once his arms were securely tied to the head of the bed, she walked over toward the fireplace and retrieved the dessert dish.

"Brownies with hot fudge sauce. Neat." She popped a corner of one of the two brownies on the plate into her mouth and chewed. "I'm going to eat just a little bit of this if it's all right with you, Max. Sexual fantasies have a way of making my blood sugar drop."

He seemed to be resisting the urge to smile.

She knew exactly what she wanted to do to him. Drive him to distraction. Bring him to his knees. Make him sexually surrender in a way that would make him completely hers, that would bind him to her forever.

In essence, do what he had done to her.

"Heh-heh."

"I don't like that little laugh," Max said. But he was finally smiling.

She brought the dessert dish to the bed, set it on the small side table.

"I think I'll need a towel for what I have planned." She headed toward the bathroom.

"They're going to wonder what the hell we've been up to in here," Max called, and she laughed. Then she came back out, towel in hand.

"We've got to get this under you, or the bed will be a complete mess and we'll have to call housekeeping in the middle of the night for clean sheets."

"This little fantasy of yours doesn't have anything to do with boiling water and needles, does it?"

"Would that make you feel better?"

"No."

She'd already maneuvered the thick towel beneath Max, and now stepped back. "You saw the movie *Speed*, didn't you?"

"Loved it," he replied, sounding a little confused. "Lots of explosions and car crashes."

Max might have been an exceptionally brilliant scientist and lecturer, but he was obviously just like any other guy when it came to movie preferences.

"Okay. Remember the dialogue? That part, what do you do? *What do you do?*"

He started to laugh.

"You're sitting in a bed, naked, with quite an impressive erection if I do say so myself. Your demented little paramour is standing by the side of the bed, chocolate sauce and whipped cream in hand. She's decided she's going to coat your body with it, especially one particular part, and slowly and voluptuously lick it off. What do you do? *What do you do?*"

Now he wasn't laughing.

HE'D ALMOST PASSED OUT from the force of his orgasm. Max could barely breathe by the time she'd gotten done with him. His heart was still pounding as she gently untied him, then took off the red silk blindfold. He slid down into bed, almost incapable of wrapping his arms around her and pressing a kiss to the top of her head.

His Eve. Such a mischief maker. So full of surprises.

"You know, Max, you're right. Sex should be fun."

He felt as if he'd run a twenty-six-mile marathon in fifteen minutes. But he forced the words up past the breathlessness in his chest.

"Marry me, Eve."

She only stared.

"It was that good?"

Even as exhausted as he was, he had to laugh.

"I'm serious."

"I know." She bit her lip, her green eyes troubled.

His heart plummeted. He'd moved too fast. Scared her. Pushed her away by his insistence on moving the relationship along faster than she wanted to.

"Well, I guess you're right," she said. "I'll have to marry you."

He relaxed. A little. "Why is that?"

"Because after doing the kinds of things we did together tonight, I can't ever see leaving you."

"Hmm." He considered this. "I should have brought out that blindfold sooner."

Eve took a deep breath, and he knew she had to confess something crucial. He stilled.

"Max, could I ask you for something and could you promise not to be too upset?"

"Yes, I do want to have your love child."

"Seriously."

Now he took her into his arms. He tightened them around her as they lay side by side in bed.

"Sure. Anything."

"Max, the woman you've slept with is not really me."

He was silent for a moment, digesting this fact.

"Are we talking alien abduction here?"

"No. No, what I mean is, ever since our one-night stand, I've been a changed woman."

"In what way?"

She took another deep breath. "You wouldn't have recognized me if you'd seen me in bed with the other guys."

"I don't think I would have been invited into the room, unless you two were into some really strange group stuff."

"No, seriously. What I mean is, you've brought out a part of me that . . . I really like. A lot."

He lifted her hair and kissed the back of her neck. "I do, too."

"And I'm . . . just starting to get comfortable with her."

He nodded his head, thinking he knew where this was headed. And not liking it.

"So if I told you that I didn't even want to *think* about marriage, but wanted to spend the next few weeks simply carrying on a hot affair, would you understand?"

She was terrified. He could sense it. Eve was avoiding the issue of commitment. Well, she could avoid it just a bit longer. But he had a feeling he was eventually going to have to force this issue with her.

The thought wasn't pleasant.

He returned to the matter at hand. "I don't believe in casual sex."

"I don't, either," she said.

"As long as we're exclusive to each other."

"Of course."

"And tons of sex. That's what a hot love affair involves." He grinned, trying to ease her out of her fear.

"Absolutely."

This he could handle. One small battle lost, but his private war, his private conquest wasn't over. Not by a long shot. He'd humor her—for now. After all, look at the short amount of time that had elapsed before the no-sex rule had been broken.

He'd win.

"Okay." Max felt himself drifting off to sleep. A badly needed sleep, because of what she'd put him through.

"Brownie?" she asked.

"No," he answered, almost half-asleep.

"Max?"

"Hmm?"

"When we wake up, can we take a bath together?"

"Yes."

He slept, the most erotic of dreams drifting through his mind. All of them starring his Eve.

THEY SPENT SATURDAY sleeping, making love, sleeping again. Neither of them left the room until check-out on Sunday. All their meals were delivered to their door, and if the owners of Swan's Bed and Breakfast thought Max and Eve went through an awful lot of towels, laughed too loud at all hours of the night or had a propensity for messy desserts full of chocolate sauce, cherry preserves and whipped cream, they never said a word.

MAX HELD EVE'S HAND all the way home Sunday night.

"That—" she sighed as they pulled into her driveway "—was the most fabulous weekend of my entire life."

"Mine, too." He kissed her. Kissed her again. Would have made love to her right out there in the car like a restless teenager if he'd thought no one was watching. But they were back at Middleton and, at Eve's request, had to be careful.

"I'll see you tomorrow night," she whispered as they broke apart after one last kiss.

"What about tonight?" he whispered back, kissing her again.

"If you spend the night with me, you won't be prepared for your first lecture."

"True." He kissed her again.

"That would be interfering with your career, and I can't in good conscience do that."

"Oh. That." He pretended to give the matter grave thought. "How about a quickie?"

She laughed. "Okay, but I'm throwing you out afterward."

Max grinned. "I love it when you talk dirty."

EIGHT WEEKS LATER, Middleton's auditorium was packed to capacity. Eve was sitting in the front row, in the seats Dr. Crummond had saved for the psychology department. She was so proud of Max. This was his evening, this was his moment, this was the last of his lecture series, and the one that was going to put him on the map at Middleton University.

Over the past few weeks, everyone she knew had complimented her on how well she looked. She'd often wondered how they would have reacted had she told them her secret.

Phenomenal sex. And plenty of it.

Her love affair with Max was going along sensationally. Though there were still moments when she sensed his frustration. Max made no secret of the fact that he wanted more. But she always forestalled any attempts he made to discuss the issue, claiming she wasn't ready.

Today she'd left for home after classes were over, having scheduled no student-teacher conferences. That gave her plenty of time to get ready, to look absolutely smashing for tonight's lecture. And the formal dinner at Dr. Crummond's house afterward.

She wanted Max to be proud of her. Several people on campus had already figured out they were a couple, and Eve had been touched by the amount of positive feedback she'd received. Even from Dr. Crummond, who had told her he thought they made quite a handsome pair indeed. She'd been tempted to tell him it had all been for Middleton.

Now, dressed in a dark blue minidress and black leather boots, with her long down coat covering her, she scanned the auditorium, looking for Max. She spotted him the instant he entered the lecture hall, and waited for him to come to her, trying to look demure. She wanted to catch him totally off guard. She still hadn't removed her coat.

He looked wonderful. His gorgeous gray suit set off his eyes and flattered his build. Max blew the image of the nerdy scientist to shreds. This elegant, sensual man made female heads turn, and probably would his entire life.

But he was clearly focused on only one female. Tonight, all of Middleton would notice. And Eve didn't even care. As long as they conducted their relationship in a way that couldn't be faulted, neither of them would be hurt professionally.

He came up to her side. "Hi."

He seemed a little distracted. She put it down to pre-performance nerves. It couldn't be easy, facing down the entire university, when so much was expected.

"Eve," Dr. Crummond boomed out, clearly unaware of the sensual vibes in the air, "why don't you show our Dr. Elliott up to the stage, perhaps get him a glass of water?" He clapped Max on the back. "I'm looking forward to your talk, Elliott. Especially the part about how you came up with that Cyber Baby. Can't wait."

"Thank you, sir."

Eve directed Max up onto the stage.

"All the sound equipment has been checked. You might want to make sure the mike's adjusted to the right height. There's ice water on the side."

The auditorium lights blinked on and off three times, the signal for everyone to stop talking and find their seats. Max set his notes on the podium, turned to Eve and smiled.

"Wish me luck."

"Oh, I do. You'll be at the dinner afterward?"

"Wouldn't miss it." He glanced out over the impressive crowd. There wasn't an empty seat, and the auditorium sat almost eight hundred people. "Anything else I should know about before I begin?"

"Other than all of Middleton is here to see you strut your stuff?"

He smiled down at her. "Brat."

She grinned up at him. "I speak the truth."

"THE FEMALE of the species," Max began, "has the ability to drive the male of that same species to distraction."

Several fraternity boys bellowed their approval. Dr. Crummond looked over his shoulder at them disapprovingly. Max continued, unfazed.

"The urge to reproduce is what drives most of us during the entire prime of our lives. That and the instinct for survival. But I'll be talking about the survival of our species in a moment, and that involves what zoologist Richard Dawkins has referred to as 'the selfish gene.'"

Eve watched his every move. Max was phenomenal. A gifted speaker, he held his audience spellbound as he slowly took them through the basic human mating ritual. He explained the frustrations all humans face in creating that most crucial, intimate bond.

"Females throughout the ages," Max continued, "have been known to use some rather ingenious methods to keep their partners in line." He glanced directly at Eve as he said this, and her heart gave a little skip. She was so proud of him.

Max paused. Took a sip of ice water. The lecture continued. No one was bored; not a cough or movement marred the excellent presentation. Eve got caught up in it herself, especially when Max briefly described his sister's plight, and how the Cyber Baby had been created. By the time he was done, several female listeners were sniffing and reaching for tissues.

"So now, near the end of the century, it's my personal belief that men need to become stronger, to take back their families, to face their responsibilities. To go beyond the limiting macho facade that the media would tell us makes up a real man."

He was compelling. Dr. Crummond was delighted. And Eve had the feeling that the evening ahead, especially Dr. Crummond's formal dinner party after the lecture, was going to be a huge success.

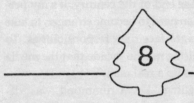

8

MAX DESCENDED from the auditorium's stage to thunderous applause. Though outwardly he knew he appeared calm, he anxiously searched the crowd for Eve, only to be waylaid by an enthusiastic Dr. Crummond.

"Brilliant lecture, my boy! This is the kind of intellectual stimulation that I like to see happening at Middleton. You gave our students a lot to think about tonight, and I thank you for that."

Max felt himself being swallowed up in a crowd of well-wishers as he scanned the auditorium for any sign of Eve.

"Where did Dr. Vaughn go?" he asked Dr. Crummond as the elderly man reached for his gray cashmere scarf and leather gloves.

"Said she'd catch a ride over to my house with Glen and Patty. Did you bring your car?"

"No, I walked."

"Better drive with me. The snow's started to come down pretty thick."

The weather proved to be ghastly. Dr. Crummond drove his ancient but reliable Oldsmobile cautiously through the campus streets until they reached his house. As they opened the door and came out of the snowstorm, the warmth from the furnace was a welcome sensation. Max gave his coat to one of the students who was helping the catering staff, then entered the living room he'd been in on New Year's Eve.

There she was. She turned, slowly, as he walked in. He was instantly aware of her, and could tell her response was the same. But as he was unsure how close she wanted them to appear at a professional gathering, Max approached the bar.

The student tending it was clearly nervous.

"Relax," Max said quietly. "You'll do fine. Most of the drinks you'll be serving tonight will be simple highballs or sodas."

The bartender was tall, blond and chunky. He blinked his pale blue eyes in astonishment. "How did you know that?"

"I bartended my way through graduate school. Could you make me a Scotch and soda?"

The young man nodded his head, then fixed the drink with admirable skill.

"To our young scientist in residence!" Dr. Crummond said, raising his voice to be heard among the chattering throng. "Your lectures have been wonderful."

HALFWAY THROUGH the formal dinner, Max was seething with masculine rage. Dr. Crummond hadn't seated him anywhere near Eve. He'd placed her directly next to a friend of his, a Dr. Alexjandro Corsino, a visiting professor from a college back east. Max especially didn't like the way Dr. Corsino was eyeing Eve's cleavage.

That dress was a stunner. Not only did the short skirt expose quite a lot of leg, but the neckline was fairly daring. Max surmised that she had to be wearing one of those push-up bras, and he liked its effect. He just didn't like the way Alexjandro Corsino was looking at her.

The worst moment of the evening had occurred just before dinner, when Dr. Corsino had—accidentally?—managed to give Eve a little pat on her rear end. Max had been shocked at the primitive urge that had erupted within him. He'd wanted to deck the guy. He hadn't felt such rage since he was sixteen and had beaten up Tommy Chadwick.

Get yourself under control.

He couldn't stop looking at her. She'd styled her hair in a way he found particularly flattering, piled up in a sexy twist on top of her head. It made him want to take those pins out, run his fingers through that auburn hair, hold her head in his hands and kiss her senseless.

He had to do something about Dr. Corsino, but what? Max was the guest of honor at this dinner; it wasn't as if he could do something unobtrusive and get away with it. And he wasn't even sure if Eve would welcome his help. He couldn't ignore the slight flash of impatience at the thought of how much easier his decision would have been if they'd been engaged.

Then he would have felt entirely justified in interfering. Hell, if he'd been engaged to Eve, Dr. Corsino probably wouldn't have made his move.

Dr. Crummond was going on and on about some subject. Max couldn't listen. He simply kept his eye on Eve and that sleazy Dr. Corsino. When Eve suddenly jumped as if she'd been bitten by a bug, Max's eyes narrowed.

Dr. Corsino apparently had a bad case of wandering hands. And Eve was especially vulnerable, what with that short skirt. Max felt totally frustrated by the limits she'd imposed on their relationship. If Dr. Corsino knew he had to deal with him.... If Max were only in a position to *protect* her—

Eve was obviously trying to escape the situation, as she stood and excused herself from the table.

Within seconds, Dr. Corsino smiled and did the same.

Max knew a rat when he saw one. Quietly, not wanting to interrupt Dr. Crummond's delighted and enthusiastic monologue, he excused himself from the formal dinner and went in search of Eve.

As HE'D SUSPECTED, Dr. Corsino was right outside the main bathroom door on the second floor of Dr. Crummond's large house, trying to get Eve to open it. She was trapped inside, and had obviously had the good sense to lock the door once she'd suspected what this man was up to.

You're at the department head's home, at a dinner in your honor. A friend of his, a house guest and distinguished gentleman in his field, though a total sleaze, is attempting to make time with the woman you love. What do you do? What do you do?

What he wanted to do was hurt the man. Badly. Teach him a lesson that he'd never forget. That a man never touches a woman unless she's given him complete approval. What had he wasted ninety minutes at the university talking about, if not male responsibility?

Max sighed. This knucklehead would never understand.

Dr. Corsino was obviously one of a breed of men who still considered women to be playthings. But Max could handle it.

"Dr. Corsino? Is something wrong?" Max adapted an attitude of helpful solicitude.

Dr. Corsino jumped, then presented Max with a rather oily, insincere smile. "Just trying to help the lady. She seems to be having a bit of trouble."

Yeah, and that bit of trouble is you.

"That's Eve in the bathroom, right?"

"Yes. A lovely woman." Dr. Corsino was shooting daggers at him with his eyes, his body language clearly asking Max to leave and let him be alone with Eve.

Not a chance.

"Honey?" Max raised his voice and deliberately injected a tone of intimacy into it. "Are you all right?"

"Max!" Eve couldn't disguise the relief in her voice.

"You are—you know—?" Now Dr. Corsino was clearly at a loss for words.

Max smiled, then lowered his voice, forcing himself to adopt a friendly manner when friendly was far from how he was feeling. "Thank you for your help and concern. I think my fiancée might be reacting badly to the dinner. She has a slight allergy to artichoke hearts, and she might have forgotten."

"Your fiancée?"

"We've been keeping it rather quiet, but yes, we plan to be married soon. This summer." *So back off, buster.*

"I see." Alexjandro clearly understood this turn of events. Max could almost see the wheels turning in the other man's head. Eve was another man's property, therefore off-limits. He couldn't lose to a woman, but would accept defeat gracefully at the hands of another man. A perceived equal.

With that, Dr. Corsino turned and faded off into the shadows where he belonged.

Max rapped softly on the door and Eve opened it instantly. He walked inside the spacious bathroom and locked the door behind him.

"Oh, Max, I've never been so glad to see you!" She quickly embraced him. "Thank you for rescuing me. I just didn't know how to handle him. He's a dear friend of Dr. Crummond's, and I didn't want to insult him—"

"You weren't upset then about what I said outside the door?"

She looked up at him. "I didn't hear anything."

"I told him you were my fiancée."

"What?"

He could feel the emotional walls starting to come up around her, and for once he didn't feel like coddling her feelings. He'd felt such utter frustration tonight while Dr. Corsino had pursued her and he'd been unable to do anything. He wanted to tell the world Eve was his. He knew it was a primitive, even immature reaction, but suddenly he felt totally resentful of the emotional limitations she continually put on their relationship.

"Are you angry?" he asked quietly.

"No," she said in a tone so low, he knew she was.

"Really?"

"Max, don't push me right now."

"Then when?" As she looked up at him, he could see she was aware he was talking about far more than what had happened tonight.

"I don't know. Look, shouldn't you be downstairs? After all, this dinner is being given in your honor—"

"Screw the dinner. And don't avoid the issue."

Silence as she faced him. He could sense her uncertainty.

"How long are you going to be scared of us, Eve? Of what we could have? Of marriage." There. He'd finally said it. Brought it out in the open. They'd have to deal with it now.

"How can you be so sure?" she whispered back, and the look on her face made him want to take her into his arms and hold her. Comfort her, not upset her. But he knew they had to face this emotional issue.

"I know what I want. I was hoping you wanted the same thing."

"I think I do, but—"

"Think isn't good enough." A part of him knew he was ruining their relationship, but another part of him had to give voice to the frustration he'd been feeling over the past weeks. "I'm not your father, Eve. I won't leave you."

The look she gave him was lethal.

"Don't," she said quietly. "Don't do this."

"Someone has to, because you aren't helping things move forward in any way."

"All of us don't come from perfect families."

He stared at her, fighting to keep his temper under control. "My family was far from perfect."

"Well they stuck around, and that gives them gold stars in my book." Eve glared up at him, and he knew she had to feel cornered. Trapped. But he wasn't prepared for the next words that came out of her mouth.

"I guess you've really summed things up, Max. I'm damaged goods. Certainly too damaged for someone like you. So I guess we'd better call it quits before we do so much emotional damage to each other, we won't be able to stand the sight of each other."

He knew what she was doing. Rejecting him before he could leave her. Trying to make the ultimate abandonment more bearable by having a small amount of control over it.

"Eve." He ran his fingers through his hair, knowing that if he made a false move now, he'd never see her again. The walls would be built too high. She'd never come out of her tower. "Eve, please."

"Don't push me. Not on this issue."

He closed his eyes, feeling more tired than he could remember. "Perhaps I was out of line." He struggled for the right words. "It was just—when I saw Dr. Corsino go after you—"

They were so far into their argument that the loud knock on the bathroom door made them both freeze.

"Hello? Eve? Max? Is everything all right?" Dr. Crummond sounded genuinely concerned.

Eve couldn't have made a sound if her life depended on it. She watched as Max, with sheer effort of will, regained control.

"I'm fine, Dr. Crummond, but I believe Eve is coming down with…a fever. Could you give us just a few minutes? Then I think I'm going to take her home."

"Certainly. I'll have your coats by the door." Then they both heard the elderly department head turn and leave.

"I can find my own way home," she said quietly.

"I'll see you home." That issue wasn't even open for discussion. Max took a deep breath. "We don't have to talk now. I'll call you in the morning. Eve, we need to discuss this."

She didn't reply. That, more than anything, told him how hurt she was by what he'd done, how he'd pushed her. He'd knowingly overstepped her private boundary lines—badly—and now didn't have a clue what to do. His frustration with their relationship had taken an aggressive turn, and he wasn't at all proud of what he'd done.

When he dropped her off at her house, she quietly said goodbye.

"I'll call you," he said.

She didn't answer.

"DR. VAUGHN?"

Eve looked up from her desk. Shelley, one of her students, stood in the doorway.

"Yes?"

"I just came by to let you know I won't be able to make my appointment this Friday. Can we reschedule?"

"Certainly."

After Shelley left, Eve continued to stare out the window at the thickly falling snow. A blizzard was being predicted, and not for the first time Eve was thankful that she lived within walking distance of her office.

It was about the only thing she was thankful for. The weather promised a disastrously prolonged winter, but nothing could match the mess she'd made of her personal life.

Max had called several times during the past few days after their argument at Dr. Crummond's, but she hadn't picked up the phone. She'd let her machine answer.

It was during moments like these, when January and February had passed and March seemed to be going on forever, that Eve wondered why she hadn't tried a little harder to get a teaching position at UCLA or USC. Even Berkeley. Sunny California, earthquakes and all, looked pretty good when you were in the middle of the dead of winter. And in the middle of a dead relationship.

Max's lecture series had finished brilliantly, even if their relationship had flamed out. From the mating dance to marriage, and then family, he had carefully taken his listeners through the experiences humans went through in the universal quest for genuine intimacy. And it was clear, from the way he was winding up the series, that Max was a man committed to family.

Eve liked that about him. Tears filled her eyes as she lowered her head onto her folded arms. Her mother would have liked Max, and where that thought had come from she had no idea. She'd wanted to talk to Patty about their five-day-old breakup, but hadn't wanted to burden her friend with her worries. She couldn't even talk to Glen; he was out of town visiting his ill brother.

When the phone rang, she jumped.

"Hello?" She'd picked it up automatically.

"Hi."

Max. She'd never get tired of listening to that gravelly, sexy voice as long as she lived. He'd finally caught her without the defense of her answering machine.

"Hi." She settled back in her chair, her heart speeding up.

"On CNN, they said a blizzard's heading this way," he told her.

"So I heard."

"It looks pretty bad outside. Do you want me to come pick you up?"

She was so thankful he had the courage to try and repair things. She'd missed him so badly, but hadn't really known how to fix the damage that had been done. Once she hadn't answered his calls, she'd really thought he would just go away. Somehow she had actually thought that would hurt less.

How wrong she'd been.

"Nah," she said. "I can get there on my own. I'm tough."

"I know that. But you don't have to be, with me."

She didn't know what to say to that.

"Did you have anything planned for dinner?" Max asked.

"No."

"Good. Then Kevin and I will make spaghetti."

She liked the way he said spaghetti, not pasta. Max, in many ways—in all the ways that counted—was a simple man.

"Sounds good. I'm leaving now."

"Be careful when you cross streets. Visibility's not all that good."

Eve hung up the phone, feeling protected and loved.

SHE WELCOMED the warmth that enveloped her as she let herself in the door of Max's house. As she wiped her feet on the mat and shook snow off her coat, cooking smells assaulted her—tomatoes, olive oil, garlic and onions. Spicy sausage. Fresh-baked bread.

The man was a whiz in the kitchen, but only with a few dishes, as he'd explained to her one evening. Spaghetti was one of them.

She found him in the kitchen. Kevin and Harley were crowded around their large dinner bowl, Harley standing beneath Kevin, her tiny black-and-white head darting out between his two large front paws as she ate. And growled. The little cat had a ferocious temper when she was hungry, and let the larger cat know it.

"Hi," she said, still nervous, then slung her coat, gloves, scarf and briefcase onto one of the kitchen chairs.

"Wine?" he said.

"Please."

He poured her a glass of very good Chianti, and she relaxed in a chair by the windows. Max's home, just down the street from hers, had the same wonderful view of the trees.

"You can hardly see the birches for the snow," she remarked, taking a sip.

"I'll bet classes will be canceled tomorrow. No one will want to be out in this mess, even walking."

"You're probably right. Middleton's pretty easy-going about snow days." Eve felt thankful for this very ordinary conversation; she wanted the chance to get on an even emotional keel with this man. They could talk about anything Max wanted to, if she could just have this little bit of peaceful time with him.

As if on cue, the phone rang. Max answered the cordless extension, so that he was free to continue the meal preparations.

"Hello? Dr. Crummond, how are you? A snow day? Eve and I were just discussing the possibility. Uh-huh. That certainly sounds reasonable."

She smiled at Max. He continued to stir the sauce.

"What am I doing? Eve and I were just going to sit down to dinner."

The man's loneliness was palpable.

"Hang on just a second, Dr. Crummond." Max covered the mouthpiece with his hand. "Could we invite him to dinner?"

She jumped at the chance to spend some time with Max with no possibility of another highly emotional argument. Dr. Crummond would serve as an excellent buffer.

"Only if he promises to be very careful on the road. It's nasty out there."

He uncovered the mouthpiece. "Would you like to join us for dinner, Dr. Crummond? It's only spaghetti, but my sauce is considered world-class."

By his quick acceptance, Dr. Crummond was so clearly pleased with the invitation that Eve's eyes stung. Once Max hung up, she moved to his cabinet to get another place setting.

"He's lonely."

Max nodded. "It's not always old age that kills people. Sometimes it's simple loneliness."

"That was a nice thing you did, Max."

"I haven't felt very nice lately."

She knew exactly what he was talking about.

"I can . . . understand why you did what you did."

"But not the way I treated you. I shouldn't have cornered you."

"You were frustrated."

"Maybe, but—"

"I'm sorry." She whispered the words in a rush. "I'm so sorry, Max, and I've missed you so much."

He stood perfectly still for a second, then came around the kitchen counter, wrapped her in his arms and held her tightly until Dr. Crummond rang the doorbell.

THE DEPARTMENT HEAD enjoyed dinner immensely. Afterward he went into Max's lab and examined everything, including how the newest Cyber Baby was coming along. He even played with Harley. The little kitten had the old man roaring with laughter over her antics.

"Why didn't I think of it before?" Max asked when they were alone in front of the TV, each with one last glass of wine in hand. They'd built a fire earlier, but now it had burned down to glowing embers.

"What?" Eve asked, wrapped comfortably in his arms.

"A cat. For Dr. Crummond. The man needs a pet. Someone to love. You saw the way he was with Harley. I'll go to the animal shelter as soon as this blizzard lets up."

"That is a truly great idea."

Max stared into the dying fire. "My mother used to call them angels in fur."

"She's right." Eve snuggled closer. "Let me know when you go, and I'll tag along."

SHE SPENT THE NIGHT with him, and as Max lay next to Eve and listened to her steady breathing, he wondered if he was making any progress at all.

She was definitely not making it easy for him.

It was so frustrating, because Max didn't see marriage as an end, only as a beautiful beginning. He knew what his parents had, what Annie and Jacques had, and he wanted the same thing for him and Eve.

He knew he could make the marriage work. They had all the necessary requisites. Chemistry, passion, attraction in spades. A sense of adventure. Humor. Commitment. Emotional maturity. Work each of them loved.

They had so much to give to each other. To the world. He was tempted to put his feelings into words, but he sensed the time just wasn't right.

She moved in her sleep, said something, her tone breathy and unsure. He slid closer, wrapped his arms around her, soothed her in her sleep. Eve stopped talking and settled into his embrace.

Max knew Eve would bloom within the structure of marriage and family. She'd feel safe and loved and cherished. He'd sensed a terrible loneliness in her that Christmas Eve. It had been deeper than her mother's death. He'd sensed Eve had been alone, fighting the world, for most of her life.

He wondered if Mary Anne Vaughn had been the same way, and doubted it. From what Eve had told him, her mother had possessed an incredible appetite for life, and had made many friends. Eve had simply been born a little more shy.

The loss of her father, before she'd even come into the world, had to have been devastating. Max couldn't comprehend never knowing your own father—or worse, realizing he hadn't wanted to stick around. As mad as Max's father had been about Annie's pregnancy, Max had never, *ever* doubted his father's love. Neither had his twin.

It had shaped both of them, just as that lack of a father had shaped Eve. She could enjoy a love affair, could enter into sexual high jinks with him, because a love affair in and of itself did not imply permanence. And if permanence was never acknowledged, there couldn't be the pain of abandonment.

Max knew there was still a crucial part of her heart Eve was keeping separate from him. And he intended to... He thought for a minute, then smiled. One thing about being a scientist, you understood male and female motives in a way most people never would.

Hell, he intended to conquer her. Completely.

THE SNOW eventually let up, and one morning early in March, Eve had an unsettling surprise. She was about to begin a lecture to her advanced seminar on human sexuality when Max and Dr. Crummond entered the back door of the lecture hall.

She wasn't exactly nervous about Max being there. Dr. Crummond attending a lecture was standard fare at Middleton. He liked keeping up with what the people in his department were doing. Unlike a lot of the elderly professors in some of the other departments, Dr. Crummond took his job seriously and refused to simply ride along on past glories.

Glen wouldn't be there; he was out of town with his brother again, who was still seriously ill, though expected to recover. Patty had offered to support her by attending, but at the last minute had called Eve and said she was feeling a little under the weather. Eve had urged her friend to stay home and take care of herself.

Max and Dr. Crummond sat toward the back, not wanting to disturb the class. Eve, at the podium, decided to pretend they weren't there. Today's lecture covered the different stages of sexuality. She usually discussed childhood and adolescence first, and already had. Now she was moving into the twenties and thirties. With all the interruptions for questions, she'd be lucky if she ever made it to the forties.

She'd heard that this particular lecture, covering the twenties, was a campus favorite, because it related directly to the lives her students were currently living.

Once everyone was settled, she began.

Eve loved to teach. One of her strongest gifts as an instructor, her professors at college had told her, was her enthusiasm for her subject. She could inject passion into anything she cared deeply about, and that passion was easily transmitted to her students. Her obvious interest ensured that her lectures were never dull or boring.

Today's topic was no exception.

She discussed where the body was in its journey through sexuality. How an individual that age was perceived by society. The tensions that came with trying to find out who you were, what you wanted to do with your life. Exploring your sexuality. The importance of birth control. The danger of sexually transmitted diseases. AIDS. Living with the knowledge that your sexuality could be an instrument in your premature death.

"In the fifties," Eve continued, warming to her subject, "all a man and woman basically worried about was getting caught. Getting pregnant outside of marriage. The stakes are much higher today, for all of us."

Cybersex. Pornography. Self-gratification. There wasn't much Eve chose to turn away from, for she had seen the damage, firsthand, of what happened when young men and women didn't have a solid sexual education.

"Of course, there's always abstinence." A smothered hoot from the side of the large lecture hall caught her attention. "No, I'm serious. There will be many cases in your lives when abstinence is a real life alternative, and probably the best one. Don't discount having that choice, as well."

The lecture was moving along splendidly. It was one she had no regrets about Dr. Crummond observing. His reports on her teaching were almost uniformly glowing. And she was pleased this was the class Max had chosen to attend, because she liked showing him what she did. She'd seen his lectures; now he would see hers.

As the lecture drew to a close, she was silently congratulating herself on its success when she was asked one last question. It threw her, but only for a second. She was sure Max was the only person in the large auditorium who noticed.

"But, Dr. Vaughn, what about love?"

She wasn't certain what the student was getting at. The girl, with wild, frizzy blond hair and wire-rimmed glasses, was sitting in the front row.

"Could you please make the question a little clearer."

"Okay. What's your opinion on love?"

She still wasn't quite sure what this young woman wanted to know. "Are you asking me if I believe in love?"

"Yes. Yes, I think I am."

Eve paused as she considered how to answer. When she did, she chose her words with care.

"I came into this profession, with this subspecialty, for a reason. I think all of us are shaped by the family we grew up in, and I was no exception."

She took a deep breath, knowing Max was in the audience and could hear every single word. Therefore, each one was vitally important.

"I saw, at a very early age, the damage love could do. How, if left unchecked, passion could destroy." She gave Max and Dr. Crummond a glance. "Those of you who attended Dr. Elliott's brilliant lecture series learned that immature passion and naive trust almost destroyed his twin sister."

She took a deep breath. Usually she didn't get this personal in a lecture, but something seemed to call for it. And she realized that she wasn't actually answering this young woman's question, but one that had been in her mind and heart for a long time.

"My mother was the seminal influence in my life."

This was harder than she'd expected. She took another breath. Her audience waited, expectant.

"My father left her before I was born. They never married. And let me say, there is no one I have ever known, in my entire life, who possessed more courage and integrity than Mary Anne Vaughn."

You could have heard the proverbial pin drop.

"She tried to pass those qualities on to me, and I like to think she succeeded." She smiled down at the young girl, who was twisting a strand of her wild, blond hair around one finger. She looked so young and unsure of herself, and Eve knew this woman deserved as honest an answer as she could give her.

"During my childhood, did I believe in love? From my mother, yes. But that love that exists between a man and a woman, that we're constantly bombarded with on television, in novels, in movies. No. I didn't. Instinct, that precious instinct for survival that Dr. Elliott explained so beautifully, kept me from believing. I couldn't believe. I was too busy surviving."

No one made a sound. Her audience seemed like a great, collective beast, leaning forward. Listening.

"Adolescence was a tortuous time for me. I was scared all the time. And I envied the girls who made it look so easy. In my twenties I buried myself in my studies. There were a few love affairs. Nothing that lasted."

"Now, in my early thirties, you ask me if I believe in love."

She kept her voice steady through great effort of will.

"You all know that scientists used to believe in the chaos theory, that all of life was chaotic and random, without a pattern. But the new physics is teaching us that there is a pattern, and it shows a great and whole world order. A *reason*."

She paused. Glanced around the huge auditorium. Smiled down at her student.

"So, the short answer to your question is—yes. I do believe in love. Absolutely."

Her audience erupted into spontaneous and heartfelt applause.

AFTERWARD, Dr. Crummond came up to the podium to congratulate her. Max remained down below, waylaid by a student.

"Excellent lecture, Dr. Vaughn."

"Thank you."

The older man sighed. "Today would have been absolutely perfect, if I hadn't heard the news about Max."

Eve went perfectly still inside.

"What news?"

"He's been offered a position at Yale. First-class. Lots of time and money for more research on the Cyber Baby. I'm sure he'll take it."

She couldn't move, or think. Or feel.

"When did this happen?"

"Last week. Didn't he tell you?"

She fumbled with her notes. Her fingers didn't seem to belong to her. She couldn't seem to make them behave. A few of her index cards scattered and she bent to pick them up. Her eyes stung.

I cannot get through this.

Max hadn't told her. And why would he? She'd made it perfectly clear to him she didn't want marriage. Was frightened of it. So he was going on with his life, a life that obviously didn't include her. Shouldn't, if she was incapable of commitment.

Damaged goods. Hadn't she even warned him?

Max was leaving her. And it was far harder than she'd ever thought any breakup in the world could be.

Now, at this moment, she realized she'd totally underestimated the impact he'd had on her life.

I won't get through this.

She would if it killed her. Yale. Of course he'd go. Who in their right mind would refuse a career opportunity like that? She couldn't expect him to turn down a chance at an Ivy League school to stay at Middleton. She hadn't exactly given him any sort of incentive to stick around.

Now, on the brink of losing him, she knew her life would never be the same. Glancing down from the stage, she saw him listening patiently to the young woman who had asked her about love. Her expression was intent as she gestured, but Eve couldn't bear to look at Max. She glanced away.

"Dr. Vaughn? Are you all right?" Now Dr. Crummond was concerned.

"Fine. Absolutely fine. I just...dropped my notes." She smiled at her department head, willing her lips to work. "I'm just tired, that's all."

At that moment, Eve knew that the drive home with Max would be one of the longest—and saddest—of her life.

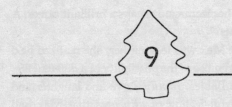

9

THEY WERE in her living room and had their coats off before she brought up his job offer. He'd congratulated her on her lecture, she'd poured them each a glass of white wine and switched on the classical music station. Bach, which matched her mood.

Coward that she was, she needed just a little more time with Max before she heard the awful truth.

Eve wanted to remember the way the winter sunshine brought out the golden brown highlights in his hair. The way his blue eyes warmed when he looked at her. She wanted that mental picture of Caliban racing into the living room and twining around his long legs.

She'd keep all these memories close to her heart, after he left.

Far harder would be remembering the way his hands felt on her body. His touch. His kiss. His scent. The absolute security she now realized she'd felt when they'd been naked in bed together. She'd never felt that secure before, and probably wouldn't ever again. Eve pictured herself as the years went by, a woman who would never marry. She would have her books, her papers, her lectures. Perhaps a brilliant career. A couple of cats.

Now that Max was leaving her, she realized he'd given her a glimpse of the possibility of a different life. A husband. Babies. *Family.* Love and laughter and that wonderful feeling of *aliveness* that Max had brought so effortlessly into her life.

But none of that was possible now.

He seemed in no hurry to leave her, and they sat on the couch, watching the winter sunshine spark the snow between the birch trees.

"I'll never get tired of that view," Max said softly, just before he kissed her. "Or this one," he added, looking down into her face.

She took a deep, steadying breath. One of them had to finish it.

"When were you going to tell me about Yale?"

His expression stilled. Slowly, moving carefully, he gave himself just enough distance from her on the couch so he could observe her.

"Dr. Crummond told you?"

"After the lecture."

"I'd asked him not to mention it to anyone. I'm sorry he did."

"Maybe it's for the best. Let me be the first to offer you my congratulations."

He studied her for a long minute. "Is that the way you really feel?"

No. I want you to tell me that you love me, that you'll never leave me, that nothing could make you go away—

"Of course I'm happy for you."

He shook his head, picked up his wineglass. "I don't want to play games about something as important as this, Eve."

"I agree. Your career—"

"I'm not talking about my career."

Her heart started to speed up. This was it. The moment. She could either be a coward and regret it for the rest of her life, or take a chance. What was it that Patty had said that day in the coffeehouse?

Sometimes you just have to take a leap of faith.

"Max, I—"

Her phone rang, the machine clicked on. Her message was short and succinct, and both of them froze when they heard the tearful plea.

"Eve? Eve, are you there? It's Patty, and . . . I think I'm having a . . . please, Eve, can you . . ."

Eve raced to her phone and picked it up.

"Patty, I'll be right there."

MAX PARKED his Porsche on the street, and Eve knew he was anticipating an ambulance needing to use the small driveway. They raced up the snow-crusted path, then found the front door locked.

Max wasted no time. He wrapped his scarf around his fist and broke one of the small panes of glass on each side of the wooden door. Then he slipped a hand inside and unlocked the door.

It didn't take them long to find Patty. She was lying on her side on the kitchen floor, and Eve bit her lip hard when she saw the blood staining the back of her friend's denim skirt.

"Max!" Patty grasped his arm as he knelt down next to her. "Oh, Max . . . I'm so . . . glad you're here." Her eyes were red-rimmed, her bottom lip trembled as he knelt down and smoothed her blond bangs off her forehead.

"Did you call for an ambulance?" he asked. Eve had never heard his voice more gentle. Her eyes stung.

"I couldn't . . . the pain . . . it came . . . too fast."

He turned to Eve and mouthed the word *call*.

She did, thankful that Patty had her address and phone number on the wall right near the phone. She wasn't sure she would have remembered. Eve answered the operator's questions as competently as she could, all the while watching Max as he held a frightened Patty in his arms and comforted her.

And wondered how she'd ever thought this man would leave anyone he loved.

After she placed the call, she sat next to Patty on the kitchen floor, near Max. Patty started to sob, fear and despair finally overtaking her. Max simply held her the way a parent would hold a frightened child. Eve stroked Patty's back. She met Max's eyes once, saw the sheen of tears and knew he had to be remembering his sister. This was a man who possessed an incredible sense of empathy.

And the man she loved with all her heart,

"Did you call Glen?" Max asked Patty.

"I can't . . . I can't . . . put him through this again." Patty hiccuped on a sob, clutching at Max's shoulder. "I was the one. He didn't . . . want to go through this again, but . . . I wanted a baby so badly—"

"Shh. Oh, Patty, it's not your fault." Max's tone was low and soothing. "Do you want me to call him?"

"No-o. I can't—"

"Okay. Okay. They should be here any minute, any minute. I want you to hold on, Patty. You've got to be strong for the baby."

She nodded her head, her shiny blond hair swinging, and Eve was struck again by how delicate her friend was. And how incredibly brave.

Faith. That was the key. Eve's mother had always taught her to respect the universe, a higher power. So now Eve did the only thing she could. She placed her hand on Patty's shoulder and began to pray. Just a simple little sentence, from the heart.

Please don't let her baby die. . . .

She heard tires crunching on snow outside. Slamming doors. Voices. Then paramedics invaded the house, laid Patty on a stretcher, then took her out the door, with Max at her side.

"I'll go with her," he said. "Can you bring the car to the hospital?"

She nodded her head, then watched as the ambulance backed out of the driveway. Red lights flashing, sirens wailing, it started down the tree-lined street.

SHE WAITED, sitting in the hard plastic hospital chair, the minutes stretching into eternity. All the while Eve prayed, placing all her trust in a higher power.

She didn't want to think about Patty's baby dying. But what this moment had done was crystallize her own problems, put things into incredible perspective.

Max was different from her father. From most men. That was probably why she'd fallen in love with him. When? Oh, if she was honest with herself, before their first night at Swan's had come to an end.

That was why she'd been so frightened.

That was why she'd run.

Watching Max on the kitchen floor with Patty had forced the biggest crack in the wall she'd always kept around her heart. She'd seen, no, *felt* the way he'd comforted her, and known at that moment he'd make a terrific husband. Father. Lover and companion.

Any little deficiencies she had would be lovingly accepted. She was all right just the way she was. He'd help her over the rough spots. This "damaged goods" business meant nothing to her Mad Max.

All of this had come to her in the quickest of flashes, and just as quickly she'd pushed this realization, this epiphany aside to think about later. Now her entire will concentrated on Patty and the fate of her unborn child.

That baby had to live. Any other outcome would be too cruel....

She got up out of the chair as she saw Max come walking down the hall. His shoulders were slumped, he looked exhausted. She could see flecks of blood on his blue chambray shirt.

He caught her eye.

Hers filled.

He gave her a quick thumbs-up.

Tears overflowed, tracking down her cheeks as she ran the last few steps down the hallway and flung herself into his arms.

"They've stabilized her. And the baby. I called Glen. He's flying home immediately. Feel up to a trip to the airport?"

She nodded her head, her heart full. Hugging him fiercely, she whispered against his ear.

"Feel up to a marriage?"

She felt the total stillness that enveloped him.

"Eve." Now he was looking down at her. "You're sure?"

She nodded her head, so full of emotion, she was unable to speak. But her expression must have told him everything he needed to know, for he caught her up against him in a crushing hug.

She was safe. And home. At last.

A few days later...

"MAX," SHE SAID sleepily from the depths of their bed at Swan's Bed and Breakfast.

"Go to sleep, Eve."

"I really like being married, Max."

"Me, too."

"All this," she whispered, so close to sleep, "from a one-night stand."

"I have a goal for this marriage," he said, sliding closer and taking her into his arms.

"What's that?"

He grinned. Eve had drunk a lot of champagne and danced and, generally, had a very good time at her wedding. They'd pulled it off in record time. At Swan's, of course, with Dr. Crummond and Glen as their two witnesses. Patty, still in the hospital, had received a blow-by-blow, extremely detailed account from her husband. And a carefully wrapped piece of their wedding cake.

"I think we should work toward a thousand and one night stands," he said, teasing her. "You know, like the Arabian Nights."

"Mmm. I like the sound of that."

He kissed the top of her head. "Go to sleep, darling."

"Uh-huh. Okay."

He couldn't resist her. Max kissed her again.

"I enjoy you, Mrs. Elliott. Immensely."

"Me, too. You, I mean. You're incredible."

She fell asleep soon after that with a contented expression on her face, and that sexy, satiated little smile made Max a very happy man indeed.

Christmas with Eve had led to a lifetime with Eve.

INSTANT WIN 4229 SWEEPSTAKES
OFFICIAL RULES

1. NO PURCHASE NECESSARY. YOU ARE DEFINITELY A WINNER. For eligibility, play your instant win ticket and claim your prize as per instructions contained thereon. If your "Instant Win" ticket is missing or you wish another, send a self-addressed, stamped envelope (WA residents need not affix return postage) to: Instant Win 4229 Ticket, P.O. Box 9045, Buffalo, NY 14269-9045 in the U.S., and in Canada, P.O. Box 609, Fort Erie, Ontario, L2A 5X3. Only one (1) "Instant Win" ticket will be sent per outer mailing envelope. Requests received after 12/30/96 will not be honored.

2. Prize claims received after 1/15/97 will be deemed ineligible and will not be fulfilled. The exact prize value of each Instant Win ticket will be determined by comparing returned tickets with a prize value distribution list that has been preselected at random by computer. Prizes are valued in U.S. currency. For each one million, or part thereof, tickets distributed, the following prizes will be made available: 1 at $2,500 cash; 1 at $1,000 cash; 3 at $250 cash each; 5 at $50 cash each; 10 at $25 cash each; 1,000 at $1 cash each; and the balance at 50¢ cash each. Unclaimed prizes will not be awarded.

3. Winner claims are subject to verification by D. L. Blair, Inc., an independent judging organization whose decisions on all matters relating to this sweepstakes are final. Any returned tickets that are mutilated, tampered with, illegible or contain printing or other errors will be deemed automatically void. No responsibility is assumed for lost, late, nondelivered or misdirected mail. Taxes are the sole responsibility of winners. Limit: One (1) prize to a family, household, or organization.

4. Offer open only to residents of the U.S. and Canada, 18 years of age or older, except employees of Harlequin Enterprises Limited, D. L. Blair, Inc., their agents and members of their immediate families. All federal, state, provincial, municipal and local laws apply. Offer void in Puerto Rico, the province of Quebec and wherever prohibited by law. All winners will receive their prize by mail. Taxes and/or duties are the sole responsibility of the winners. No substitution for prizes permitted. Major prize winners will be asked to sign and return an Affidavit of Eligibility within 30 days of notification. Noncompliance within this time or return of affidavit as undeliverable may result in disqualification, and prize may never be awarded. By acceptance of a prize, winners consent to the use of their names, photographs or other likeness for purposes of advertising, trade and promotion on behalf of Harlequin Enterprises Limited, without further compensation, unless prohibited by law. In order to win a prize, residents of Canada will be required to correctly answer a time-limited arithmetical skill-testing question to be administered by mail.

5. For a list of major prize winners (available after 2/14/97), send a self-addressed, stamped envelope to: "Instant Win 4229 Sweepstakes" Major Prize Winners, P.O. Box 4200, Blair, NE 68009-4200, U.S.A.

MILLION DOLLAR SWEEPSTAKES
OFFICIAL RULES
NO PURCHASE NECESSARY TO ENTER

1. To enter, follow the directions published. Method of entry may vary. For eligibility, entries must be received no later than March 31, 1998. No liability is assumed for printing errors, lost, late, non-delivered or misdirected entries.

   To determine winners, the sweepstakes numbers assigned to submitted entries will be compared against a list of randomly, preselected prize winning numbers. In the event all prizes are not claimed via the return of prize winning numbers, random drawings will be held from among all other entries received to award unclaimed prizes.

2. Prize winners will be determined no later than June 30, 1998. Selection of winning numbers and random drawings are under the supervision of D. L. Blair, Inc., an independent judging organization whose decisions are final. Limit: one prize to a family or organization. No substitution will be made for any prize, except as offered. Taxes and duties on all prizes are the sole responsibility of winners. Winners will be notified by mail. Odds of winning are determined by the number of eligible entries distributed and received.

SWP-H12CFR

3. Sweepstakes open to residents of the U.S. (except Puerto Rico), Canada and Europe who are 18 years of age or older, except employees and immediate family members of Torstar Corp., D. L. Blair, Inc., their affiliates, subsidiaries, and all other agencies, entities, and persons connected with the use, marketing or conduct of this sweepstakes. All applicable laws and regulations apply. Sweepstakes offer void wherever prohibited by law. Any litigation within the province of Quebec respecting the conduct and awarding of a prize in this sweepstakes must be submitted to the Régie des alcools, des courses et des jeux. In order to win a prize, residents of Canada will be required to correctly answer a time-limited arithmetical skill-testing question to be administered by mail.

4. Winners of major prizes (Grand through Fourth) will be obligated to sign and return an Affidavit of Eligibility and Release of Liability within 30 days of notification. In the event of non-compliance within this time period or if a prize is returned as undeliverable, D. L. Blair, Inc. may at its sole discretion, award that prize to an alternate winner. By acceptance of their prize, winners consent to use of their names, photographs or other likeness for purposes of advertising, trade and promotion on behalf of Torstar Corp., its affiliates and subsidiaries, without further compensation unless prohibited by law. Torstar Corp. and D. L. Blair, Inc., their affiliates and subsidiaries are not responsible for errors in printing of sweepstakes and prize winning numbers. In the event a duplication of a prize winning number occurs, a random drawing will be held from among all entries received with that prize winning number to award that prize.

5. This sweepstakes is presented by Torstar Corp., its subsidiaries and affiliates in conjunction with book, merchandise and/or product offerings. The number of prizes to be awarded and their value are as follows: Grand Prize — $1,000,000 (payable at $33,333.33 a year for 30 years); First Prize — $50,000; Second Prize — $10,000; Third Prize — $5,000; 3 Fourth Prizes — $1,000 each; 10 Fifth Prizes — $250 each; 1,000 Sixth Prizes — $10 each. Values of all prizes are in U.S. currency. Prizes in each level will be presented in different creative executions, including various currencies, vehicles, merchandise and travel. Any presentation of a prize level in a currency other than U.S. currency represents an approximate equivalent to the U.S. currency prize for that level, at that time. Prize winners will have the opportunity of selecting any prize offered for that level; however, the actual non U.S. currency equivalent prize if offered and selected, shall be awarded at the exchange rate existing at 3:00 P.M. New York time on March 31, 1998. A travel prize option, if offered and selected by winner, must be completed within 12 months of selection and is subject to: traveling companion(s) completing and returning of a Release of Liability prior to travel; and hotel and flight accommodations availability. For a current list of all prize options offered within prize levels, send a self-addressed, stamped envelope (WA residents need not affix postage) to: MILLION DOLLAR SWEEPSTAKES Prize Options, P.O. Box 4456, Blair, NE 68009-4456, USA.

6. For a list of prize winners (available after July 31, 1998) send a separate, stamped, self-addressed envelope to: MILLION DOLLAR SWEEPSTAKES Winners, P.O. Box 4459, Blair, NE 68009-4459, USA.

EXTRA BONUS PRIZE DRAWING
NO PURCHASE OR OBLIGATION NECESSARY TO ENTER

7. The Extra Bonus Prize will be awarded in a random drawing to be conducted no later than 5/30/98 from among all entries received. To qualify, entries must be received by 3/31/98 and comply with published directions. Prize ($50,000) is valued in U.S. currency. Prize will be presented in different creative expressions, including various currencies, vehicles, merchandise and travel. Any presentation in a currency other than U.S. currency represents an approximate equivalent to the U.S. currency value at that time. Prize winner will have the opportunity of selecting any prize offered in any presentation of the Extra Bonus Prize Drawing; however, the actual non U.S. currency equivalent prize, if offered and selected by winner, shall be awarded at the exchange rate existing at 3:00 P.M. New York time on March 31, 1998. For a current list of prize options offered, send a self-addressed, stamped envelope (WA residents need not affix postage) to: Extra Bonus Prize Options, P.O. Box 4462, Blair, NE 68009-4462, USA. All eligibility requirements and restrictions of the MILLION DOLLAR SWEEPSTAKES apply. Odds of winning are dependent upon number of eligible entries received. No substitution for prize except as offered. For the name of winner (available after 7/31/98), send a self-addressed, stamped envelope to: Extra Bonus Prize Winner, P.O. Box 4463, Blair, NE 68009-4463, USA.

© 1994 HARLEQUIN ENTERPRISES LTD.
This sweepstakes is not associated with any State Lottery.

SWP-H12CF1

As Seen on TV!

Free Gift Offer

With a Free Gift proof-of-purchase
from any Harlequin® book, you can receive
a beautiful cubic zirconia pendant.

This stunning marquise-shaped stone is a genuine cubic
zirconia—accented by an 18" gold tone necklace.
(Approximate retail value $19.95)

Send for yours today...
compliments of ◆HARLEQUIN®

To receive your free gift, a cubic zirconia pendant, send us one original proof-of-purchase, photocopies not accepted, from the back of any Harlequin Romance®, Harlequin Presents®, Harlequin Temptation®, Harlequin Superromance®, Harlequin Intrigue®, Harlequin American Romance®, or Harlequin Historicals® title available in August, September or October at your favorite retail outlet, together with the Free Gift Certificate, plus a check or money order for $1.65 u.s./$2.15 can. (do not send cash) to cover postage and handling, payable to Harlequin Free Gift Offer. We will send you the specified gift. Allow 6 to 8 weeks for delivery. Offer good until December 31, 1996, or while quantities last. Offer valid in the U.S. and Canada only.

Free Gift Certificate

Name: _____

Address: _____

City: _____ State/Province: _____ Zip/Postal Code: _____

Mail this certificate, one proof-of-purchase and a check or money order for postage and handling to: HARLEQUIN FREE GIFT OFFER 1996. In the U.S.: 3010 Walden Avenue, P.O. Box 9071, Buffalo NY 14269-9057. In Canada: P.O. Box 604, Fort Erie, Ontario L2Z 5X3.

FREE GIFT OFFER   084-KMFR

ONE PROOF-OF-PURCHASE
To collect your fabulous FREE GIFT, a cubic zirconia pendant, you must include this original proof-of-purchase for each gift with the properly completed Free Gift Certificate.

084-KMFR

You're About to Become a *Privileged Woman*

Reap the rewards of fabulous free gifts and benefits with proofs-of-purchase from Harlequin and Silhouette books

Pages & Privileges™

It's our way of thanking you for buying our books at your favorite retail stores.

PROOF OF PURCHASE HT-PP20

Offer expires March 31, 1997

**Harlequin and Silhouette—
the most privileged readers in the world!**

For more information about Harlequin and Silhouette's PAGES & PRIVILEGES program call the Pages & Privileges Benefits Desk: 1-503-794-2499

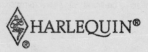

HARLEQUIN®

HT-PP20